MY COLD MAD FATHER

MY COLD MAD FATHER
First Edition

ISBN: trade paper 978-1940999-31-9
© 2018 Somtow Sucharitkul

Diplodocus Press
Bangkok • Los Angeles

0 9 8 7 6 5 4 3 2 1
First Edition

MY COLD MAD FATHER

stories about fathers and sons

S.P. SOMTOW

LOS ANGELES· BANGKOK

diplodocus

"And it's old and old it's sad and old it's sad and weary I go back to you, my cold father, my cold mad father, my cold mad feary father, till the near sight of the mere size of him, the moyles and moyles of it, moananoaning, makes me seasilt saltsick and I rush, my only, into your arms."

— *Finnegans Wake*

TO MY FATHER
ON HIS SIXTIETH BIRTHDAY

Introduction to the Introduction

Years ago …

Decades, in fact, there was a wonderful publishing house called Pulphouse. They produced all sorts of incredible books through a peculiar system that was, in essence, xerox. This was before print on demand, before Createspace, before anyone could publish anything for free on Amazon.com, and it was a bunch of enthusiastic people in the American Northwest putting out books in hardback, in limited editions, and in trade paper through a clever system that just kept them coming.

They were all my friends, the people running that organization, and I came to publish several books with them. The clever one-story chapbooks, all with uniform covers — I did one of those. The novellas published as limited editions — check. The weekly magazine that lasted a dozen issues — check. The annual magazine in hardcover format — check.

Then there was the series of single-author collections, each containing 30,000 words selected by the author and with a uniform cover portraying the writer, all drawn by, I believe, George Barr. I signed up for that, too.

I'm not quite sure what happened to Pulphouse, but they contrived to go out of business just as my collection was about to come out — I had already corrected the proofs.

I dedicated the book to my father on his 60th birthday, though none of the relationships in this novel are anything like my relationship with him. The 60th is a very special birthday for Thais, because it combines a ten year "decimal system" cycle with the astrological cycle of twelve "animal" years. Amazingly, my Dad is now 86 so this comes a little late.

The title of the collection, which comes from Finnegans Wake, *also has nothing to do with my real father, of course. As with everything else in* Finnegans Wake, *I'll be damned if I know what it means, but it is so cool!*

INTRODUCTION

This is a collection of short stories from throughout my career. The earliest, *Fire from the Wine-dark Sea*, is the first fantasy story I ever wrote, and dates from 1978; the most recent, *Darker Angels*, was composed only a few months ago as I write these words in the week before Thanksgiving, 1991. Each of the stories deals, in one way or another, with the relationship between fathers and sons. It is a theme that I've treated in many of my novels as well, such as the recent *riverrun*, and one which, for one reason or another, seems to have obsessed me, though it is by no means the only theme around which a collection like this could have been built.

For example, I toyed with putting together a book of "stories about theology and zombies." I actually *do* have enough stories about this rather recondite combination of subjects to fill a collection of this size ... from the Stoker-nominated *ResurrechTech™* to *Darker Angels*, which does appear here under a different rubric. Another possibility would have been stories about weird art forms;

another, stories about women in peril in the Far East. Or exotic Asian stories in general.

But the stories in this collection are very personal for me — not because they are particularly autobiographical, or because they are set in backgrounds with which I'm familiar, but simply because I have a father — I don't have any sons as yet — and he and I come from a family whose dynamics and interactions are almost entirely dominated by the women in it.

I've had a lot of women in my life ... sisters, cousins, aunts, grandmothers, great-aunts, and an exceptionally charismatic great-grandmother ... not to mention my mother, to whom I owe my enduring love of the horror genre, for it was she who took me to see performance after performance of *Psycho* when I was a child. Perhaps it's been easier for me to write about women than it might be for a person brought up in the Judaeo-Christian-Moslem culture in which the two sexes really do inhabit entirely different universes.

Because I've spent a greater proportion of my life observing women in positions of authority and power than I suspect most American men have, I've naturally tended to use female protagonists, and write about women, more than many of my male colleagues in American fiction. My first novel, *Starship and Haiku*, my longest novel, *Moon Dance*, and my most notorious novel, *Vampire Junction*, are all told in large measure from a female perspective. This may sound trivial, but one of my proudest moments was being told by a female reader that she had become sexually aroused to the point of orgasm in reading a passage from *Moon Dance* written from the female viewpoint. We arrogantly expect women to be able to write convincingly about male perspectives, but when the reverse occurs it is often subjected to the dancing bear syndrome. So I wasn't offended at all by this lady's comment — I was profoundly flattered.

Not that I've succumbed to Robert Bly-ism in my old age, but this book, by contrast, is about guys. Fathers and sons in particular, and also about the way fathers and sons perceive the mysterious other partner in the Oedipal triad. In these four stories, the wife-mother figure appears more as an icon than a human character — in two cases she is dead, in the other two she is more of a mythic figure than a real one. The stories speak of the rivalry between father and son; the difficulty of expressing love; rebellion and forgiveness; the sacrifices, pains, and bitter-sweetnesses of this most special bond.

As I write these words, my father is just about to turn sixty. In Thailand, this is concerned the end of the fifth great astrological cycle, and it's a year of great auspiciousness. My father has never been like any of the fathers in this book, but I have no doubt he has experienced some of their conflicts, their emotions. The words of James Joyce in the epigraph to this book — part of which I also used as the epigraph to my novel *riverrun* — express far better than I can the complex feelings my relationship with my father arouses is me.

I hope he enjoys this birthday tribute ... and that he won't think I'm using any of these stories to write about *him!*

KINGDOMS IN THE SKY

I wrote this story after many years of reading occasional newspaper reports about present-day children found sacrificed at the peaks of Peruvian mountains. This led to a deep interest in the culture of the Incas and to my halting study of the Quechua language, and finally into an orgy of research into modern Peru.

The Abraham and Isaac story has its counterpart in every mythos, but the Buddhist fable of Prince Vessandara, which is narrated at the center of this story, has a completely different "take" on the archetype than does the Judæo-Christian version — which profoundly underscores the difference between the two great cultures which nurtured me.

abhisandhaya tu phalam
dambhartham api caiva yat
ijyate bharata-srestha
tam yajnam viddhi-rajasam

But that sacrifice which is undertaken for gain,
Or from pride, O King of the Bharatas,
that sacrifice partakes of the nature of passion.

—Bhagavad-Gita

Kingdoms in the Sky

All I ever wanted was an endless summer of thrashing and tagging the L-train and scamming with chicks. Those were the days when I went to public school and my friends didn't know I had money. They didn't know I got picked up by a dude in a uniform in a white limo when I got off at my stop. I'd give anything to have those days back.

On first day of summer vacation and me and my friends were skating along the abandoned sewer. There's this big pipe that we use as a makeshift ramp and we practice our tagging on the walls too plus at night we bring girls over sometimes. On this particular day I'm taking a three-sixty too fast and find myself skidding out of control down the incline. A man in a black suit is waiting for me at the other end. My friends didn't know who it was so they stayed away, thinking, you know, the law maybe.

But I'm all, "Hi, Enzo." Enzo was like our chauffeur.

"We gotta go somewhere, Tony. Your Dad wants you. Right now." He started to take the skateboard from me to put in the trunk. "Good clothes are in the limo."

We drove off. I changed into good clothes. I thought we were going back to the mansion up in Oak Park but instead we were looping alongside the lake, toward the Field Museum. We have our own wing there, the Severini Collection, which is all stuff we brought back from South America. I never thought of it as laundering until I read the article in last week's *Sun-Times*. The one about my dad and the FBI.

So Enzo walks me over to the Collection and there's my Dad. In the first room of our wing there's nothing except one glass case and in it there's a pair of hands — solid gold hands. The caption reads: *Funerary Gloves — Inca — gift of Rodolfo Severini.* Dad was standing there looking at the hands and his hands were folded just like the golden hands that had been taken off some dead dude, who'd lain in the ground untouched for like five hundred years.

I'm all, "Dad, it's me."

He turned. "Tony." He looked dashing in his Armani suit with his twirled mustache. It was like 100° outside but he managed to look pretty cool.

"You sent for me?"

"All in good time. Come on, son, let's look at some of these treasures ... yeah, let's feast our eyes." His own eyes were sad. I could tell that he was trying to hide something. Maybe he was thinking of Mom, who is someone I don't even remember too well anymore.

"Feeling kinda down, huh, Dad.   Cares of the business getting to you."

"You can read my mind."

Okay, so it wasn't as much fun as graffitiing a wall, but I could deal with Inca art treasures for one afternoon. Dad put his hand on my shoulder and steered me into the next room. It was full of pottery with geometric designs and statues with staring eyes.

"Look at that one, it's grotesque ... the bulging eyes, the fat hips ..." he said.

"Big dick, though," I said.

"Look at that!" It was a row of tapestries — some with abstract patterns, some that showed weird little guys dancing around.

"Look at *that!*" A stream ran through the hallway and there was this model of a sailing ship made from reeds and like these tall wax dudes in flowing robes and hanging earlobes and gigantic headdresses standing around gesturing, and behind it all a wall painting that showed a massive pyramid peering from a mass of foliage, and behind that mountains capped with snow.   "They must've added that since last summer."

"Yeah, there's a lot of new stuff," Dad said. He led me down a corridor toward a room I'd never seen before. It was cordoned off, but the guard let us through. A sign read: *huaca* — *an Inca sacred place — reconstructed environment.*

The place was built to look like a cave with big plaster boulders. The airconditioning was really blasting here and the cold felt good. The floor sloped upward steeply. Here and there, in a niche in the rock, you could see a statuette or a display of gold jewelry.

"Come on," said Dad. He loped uphill, helping me up by the hand. His palm was sweating. We reached a stone staircase — fake stone that is — that led up to an inner cave. It was walled off with plexiglass and light hit it in such a way that you couldn't see inside until your nose was practically rubbing against it. The temperature became noticeably cooler and I was shivering when I got there.

Inside the hollow, seated on a stone plinth, was a dead boy. He was nude. He was cross-legged and his hands were folded on his lap kind of the way the funerary gloves were folded in the antechamber. He was young, my age I guessed. He was perfectly preserved. I mean, I stood there waiting for him to breathe, holding my own breath, until I couldn't hold it anymore and fogged the plexiglass with my gasp.

"Who is he?" I said.

"Human sacrifice," my Dad said. "They left him in a little temple on top of a mountain in the Andes. Offered him to Wiraqocha, creator of the universe, I expect. That's how the High Inca kept the empire together — with treaties between himself and all the subsidiary kingdoms, sealed by the mutual exchange of children for sacrifice."

"Weird." I couldn't look away from the dead kid. He was covered in gold: gold armbands, gold neck-chain, gold anklets, gold headdress. There were icicles on the walls. Real ones. I guess they had to keep it below freezing in there to keep him from going bad. He was good-looking, in spite of his geeky hair with its pageboy bangs.

"Probably," Dad said, "the son of someone important ... look at how aristocratic he looks ... he's sitting there and his eyes seem to say, 'Look at me guys, worship me, I'm king of the sky.'"

"Not for me," I said. "I think he's saying more like, 'You assholes ... I wanted to spend the summer tagging the L-train and scamming chicks ... and you've made me into a god and I'm bored out of my fucking mind."

Dad laughed. "You'd know better than me," he said. "You're the one who's part Inca ."

But I didn't really hear him because I was looking into the dead boy's face. I've seen Egyptian mummies but he wasn't like that. He was someone *real*. His lips were parted like he was about to say something. I got the feeling that if I stood there long enough, we were going to start communicating.

Sometimes I would get that feeling with my brother Matt, but it was not intense like that. With Matt, you *knew* that he was never going to speak. But with the dead boy I wasn't sure. It was magical and beautiful and terrifying.

I knew I was never going to forget him.

"Come on, son," Dad said. He turned me around and began to walk me downhill. I got the feeling he wanted to get out of there as fast as he could. "Pizza at Armand's, huh?"

"Hey, Dad, let me look some more."

"*Basta.* I'm going away tomorrow. There's trouble. The business ... you know."

"Can I come? I never get to go on your business trips. You always bring back these rad gifts, you tell me stories, but you never take me. I want to see the jungles, the mountains, the cocaine fields, the —"

"You really mean it, son?"

Then all of a sudden my Dad hugs me hard — I'm not used to that — and it's like he's never going to see me again. And there are tears in his eyes but he looks away in the nick of time, he thinks, so I won't see them.

I'm all "Shit, Dad," and then he looked kinda embarrassed so he just said, "The servants have already packed your things."

He started to walk away but I had to run back to steal another glance at the dead boy.
***

The bad part was that my brother Matt was coming too and that meant bringing his babysitter Lisa, who can only be described as a geek. She was a real doctor, though, which meant she could prescribe anything we needed at the drop of a hat. I don't know how much it costs to buy a doctor, but she was always letting us know, in subtle ways, that she could be making more money in some fancy clinic, even though as part of the household staff she never had to do anything except watch TV and write prescriptions.

We got into Lima and were whisked off to a Sheraton some suburb. It was no different from home except for the funny money. There was a pool, a private jacuzzi in our penthouse suite, a great view of suburban sprawl that might as well have been Schaumburg or Barrington. Dad took meetings all day and the three of us were cooped up in the suite, binging on room service.

Matt was just like me — he had jet-black hair and arched eyebrows and was kind of compact — a year older, but he could have been my twin brother. Except he had never talked. He wasn't a retard and he wasn't deaf. He just didn't speak. Well, to me sometimes, but only in my dreams. Or daydreams.

We were playing monopoly and watching cable and wolfing down *ceviche,* which is sort of Peruvian sushi. In our version of monopoly, I moved all the pieces around, Lisa sat around complaining, and Matt sat around sorting the green and red plastic houses into pretty piles. If this is what visiting an exotic country is like, I was thinking, send me back to the Field Museum.

That's when we were sent for.

"Time to go, Matt." He looked up when I said his name. I helped him get dressed. Lisa came downstairs with us, toting her medicine bag.

Driving through town was the only time we really saw Lima. We saw shantytowns sprouting out of the dirt alongside the highway, cramped and treeless, with bullfight posters flapping on walls of adobe or galvanized iron ... we inched our way through tiny streets with colonial buildings and hordes of shrieking kids ... the Plaza de Armas with the cathedral and Pizarro's crypt, thronged with tourists and hustlers swarming over a concrete desert with a few parched oases of greenery. There were even thrashers in the square, riding rings around one of the fountains. But the three of us were sitting in our sealed antiseptic limo and we could see but we couldn't touch, hear, smell. At last I couldn't stand it any more and I rolled down the window.

It was getting on toward sunset and we began driving toward the sun so I knew we were bound for the shore. It was humid but not stifling the way it can be in summer back home. There was like this dirty fog over everything. The driver told us it was called *guara*. The air smelled like fish and salt and gasoline fumes and used tampax and exotic flowers. The hubbub along the sidewalks was partly Spanish but partly a softer language — Quechua they called it — liquid and rhythmical.

We went through districts called San Isidro and Miraflores. Then the limo stopped at a district called Barranco. Kind of a hippie or beatnik place. A steep tree-lined street snaked down toward the sea. The driver pointed. "The Bridge of Sighs," he said proudly. Guitar music poured out of coffee shops and dudes with high cheekbones wrapped in colorful blankets sat around playing wooden flutes — there was even a llama tethered to a gate, so the whole place shrieked *tourist tourist* at us.

A seedy dude tries to attract Matt's attention but I pull him sharply towards us. "Pusher!" I tell him. "You know how Dad hates pushers!"

The driver led us up some stone steps to a room above a coffee shop. The doorway was guarded by stone Incas. It smelled of beer and tobacco. Inside there were old guys sitting around in dark suits. The shades were all down and the room was lit by candlelight. My Dad was there too … on a special kind of chair, raised up on a dais … he was like a king among these people. God I was proud of him.

There was an old Indian woman in the shadows. When she saw us she kind of pounced and starting covering my face with kisses. I recoiled and she began muttering, *"Antonio, Antonio, ¿no me quieres?"* and then she started to babble in Quechua. She stepped back in a huff, cocked her head to look quizzically at Matt, and then slunk away when she heard my father talking.

"Tony," Dad said, "you're here. I want you to meet Dr. José von Steinberg … Alfonso Ortega y Muñoz … Gabriel de la Verdad … Porfirio Knightley from our Argentine office … Captain Buenaventura of the PIP, that's the Peruvian FBI, but he's all right, he's a *compadre* … oh, and this is Juanito, Señor

Ortega's son — he may be joining us next summer in Chicago."

Then I saw this kid, about my age I guessed, who'd been sitting in the dark corner with the old woman. He got up and held out his hand and walked toward me, stiffly, with the floorboards creaking. He was littler than me. He was a fraidy-cat; I just stared him in the eye and he wouldn't come any closer.

"I am sure you will be getting along superbly," said Señor Ortega, a skeletal man with a cigar. "And you, Tony, you look to be like the perfect *capacocha*. You do us honor."

There was a burst of murmuring at his words. Some people seemed upset. My Dad was trying to look calm. I didn't know what they were talking about, so I didn't answer. But something had come over Matt. He came up real close to me and was squeezing my hand over and over, which meant he was frightened.

Oblivious, Señor Ortega went on: "To have a kingdom here on earth — as your father does — what a splendid thing! — but to have a kingdom in the sky, a kingdom forever — is that not more magnificent still? — is that not what you desire?"

"No way," I said. "I'm a down-to-earth kinda guy."

For some reason, my words caused an uproar. Only the Indian woman seemed pleased. My Dad turned to them and berated them all in Quechua. That surprised me. I didn't know he could speak it.

At length, Ortega turned to me and said, "I am sorry, *capacocha*. But we are all one *ayllu* here. Our dreams are as one man's dream." He downed a whole glass of *chicha* beer in one gulp.

Something was *really* bothering Matt now. He wouldn't let go of me. He was making gurgling noises. There was stark terror in his eyes. I just knew he was going to shit himself — that was his way of getting out attention.

"Lisa," I said, "you gotta give him something *right now*." She rooted around in her back for a pill or a hypodermic, and I said, "Dad, what's going on?"

My father said, "We're going on a journey. You wanted to see the cocaine fields? We're going there. But first you have to let Dr. von Steinberg look at you. We want to make sure you're well enough for the trip."

"Come with me, Dad," I said.

So he takes me into an inner room and the PIP man stands at the door curtain with his AK-47. Dr. von Steinberg prods at me and looks at my teeth. Then he measures each one of my fingers with calipers and uses a tape measure to figure out the distance from my wrist to halfway up my forearm. He writes it all down in a book, then he says, "Would you mind undressing now, Tony?"

I don't like the way this is going. I'm starting to panic. I'm all, "Dad, I know you're into a lot of shady shit, but if you're branching out into kiddie porn, I don't want anything to do with it."

Dad smiled a wan smile. "Do what he says, *ragazzino*. It won't hurt."

So I'm all standing in the middle of this room with no clothes on. It's drafty and the room stinks of salt water and chemicals. I'm shivering my butt off.

"You have a mole on left shoulder," Dr. von Steinberg said. It sounded like an accusation.

"So? Had it for years."

"I will remove it. *Capacocha* must be perfect." He pulls out this big old *device* from like this file cabinet and plugs it in, and it sounds like *dzzzt! dzzzt!* like a Frankenstein machine, and I'm all, "Don't do that! It's gonna hurt!"

Dad nodded. I got the feeling for a moment that he was in too deep, that things were out of his control. He wouldn't look it me.

"You will feel nothing," Dr. von Steinberg said, "just a leedle prick, like the bite of an ant—"

"*Yeeoow!*"

"Is done."

Then Dr. von Steinberg fell to his knees in front me me — a shivering stark naked eighth grader from Illinois— and he's all, "You are without blemish. Thank you for coming to us. Without you we are nothing."

I look up and the dude from the PIP is on his knees too. There's just me and my Dad standing and he won't look into my eyes.

They didn't give me my old clothes back, but threw a cloak over me. It smelled of old sweat and weird spices and it was all embroidered like those tapestries at the Field. It was fastened with a solid gold brooch. I kept saying, "What's going on?" but no one would say anything. It was almost like they were afraid of me, of my power.

We went into the main room and they were all applauding, except the old Indian woman who had Juanito in her arms and was rocking him and singing in a cracked voice. Matt was out cold on a bench. Lisa must have OD'd him.

Juanito comes up to me. He's holding out a gift. It's a Game Boy and some cartridges. He whispers something in Quechua with his eyes downcast. Then, one by one, they're all piling up gifts on the floor. Bundles of 10,000 *inti* banknotes, a portable television, a battered box of Hydrox cookies —

I stood like a dummy, trying to smile.

"Well," said Dad, "better get the show on the road, I guess."

Silently we filed out and went downstairs. A convoy of limousines was waiting for us. I followed my Dad into an even bigger limo than the one we'd come on. Lisa had to carry Matt. The PIP man came with us. He sat at attention, clutching his AK-47.

There was no one in the streets. There's a curfew in Lima. The police were setting up a roadblock just ahead of us. "How can we go anywhere, Dad?" I said.

"It's okay, *ragazzino*, we own these police and they've given us all *salvos conductos*."

We pulled away. It was night. We turned south, down the Pan-American Highway. We drove fast. I was happy to have the new Game Boy and got engrossed in a Mario Brothers game. I didn't know where we were going but I was glad to get out of that smoky place. Our limo was out front and I could see the lights of the others when I peered out the back window. We were the only people on the coastal desert road.

After a while I noticed my Dad looking at me funny, like he didn't want me to know he was looking at me. I stopped the game even though it was a level I'd never reached before. On the right was the sea and on the left were distant snowy peaks lit up by moonlight. Here and there a shack stood by the road. The PIP man was all rigid, ready to fire. I guess he was like our bodyguard.

I'm all, "Dad, those friends of yours ... I don't know. That Ortega dude gives me the creeps."

"Go easy on him son, he's your *padrino*, you know."

"My godfather? Him?"

"And one of the richest men in South America."

"And who's the old woman?"

"You'll find out." He fiddled with some controls and the TV came on. It was an episode of *I Love Lucy*, dubbed in Spanish. Then he helped himself to a champagne. He was more depressed than I'd ever seen him.

"So how bad can it be?" I said. "Maybe those Shining Path guerilla dudes have taken over a few fields, maybe the Americans are trying to buy them off, but ... you still got us, me and Matt ... always, Dad."

"Are you feeling hyper? You want Lisa to give you a Valium?"

"No, Dad."

My nose to the window, I'm all watching the road unreel ... mountains and more mountains to the east ... now and then a bus roaring past, garishly decorated, with people hanging out of the windows ... a lone peasant on horseback leading a couple of llamas ... a flock of sheep ... and everywhere the silvery moonlight, making the foliage glow like polished onyx ... I'm all hypnotized by the limo's smooth motion and Matt's shallow breathing and the sound of Lisa's voice as she and Dad talk about boring things like the drug war and the economic indicators and the plane schedule. I don't need a Valium to put me to sleep....

***

I know I'm dreaming when I hear Matt talking to me. Matt's standing beside me in the Field Museum in the room with the dead boy and we both have our noses pressed against the plexiglass. But the cave's all huge now and you can hear the wind screaming outside.

Matt's saying, "You want to go in there? You want to be king of the sky?"

Okay, so the glass starts to dissolve and becomes this fine mist and suddenly we're through. At first I think the dead boy's going to come to life ... I'm afraid of that … afraid it's going to be one of those horror movie kind of dreams … and I'll wake up sweating. But no. He's dead and he never moves.

I see the old Indian woman scurrying into the shadows.

"Who is she, Matt?" I say.

"You know," he says. I put out my hand and touch the dead boy. He's cold and dry. I feel the warmth siphon out of my fingers. "Is he dead, Tony?" Matt says. "Is he a god or is he just a dead thing on a mountain peak? I have to know, Tony! Otherwise I won't be able to make up my mind...."

"About what?" The wind whistles.

"I'm scared, Tony," Matt says. I turn to him. His lips don't move when he talks, of course — I can only hear him inside my head — but I can see from his eyes that he's never been so scared in his life. "People out there think, just because I can't talk, I don't know what's going on. But I know even better than you do sometimes, little brother. Don't let them do it to me —"

"No one's gonna do anything to you, Matt … it's okay … like I'm here, Matt, I'm *here.*"

But I get the feeling he doesn't believe me. That's why I start shaking him and he rattles like a jumble of bones in a knapsack and he turns to dust that slips through my fingers and the dead boy smiles and slowly, slowly, slowly cranes his neck with a *crick-crick-crick* ratcheting straight out of *The Exorcist.*

And then I hear this thundering and I know we're in the middle of an avalanche and the cavern's going to collapse on itself and as I try to run away the plexiglass condenses out of the mist and I'm banging my head against it, *bang bang bang*
***

bang against the window of the limousine.

We weren't on the highway anymore, that was for sure. I woke up all at once. The limousines were bumping and lurching. Gravel pelted us. The Andes loomed ahead, impossibly huge. There was jungle on either side of us. Banana trees. Orchids. Even with the airconditioning you could feel the moisture in the air, heavy with the fragrance of ripe mangoes and rotting vegetation. Peru will do that to you. Blink once and you've gone from temperate to tropical.

"Better pull yourself together, son," Dad says. "It's Sunday. Can't miss mass. Lisa, get out some decent clothes for Tony."

And just like that we're coming out of the jungle into a broad clearing at the foot of a mountain. The top is in the clouds and all snowy but down we're drenched in sunlight. The lower part of the mountain's like one giant green staircase. The terraces were carved into the hillside 2,500 years ago, Dad says, and they've always been used for coca growing. "And look up there." Coiling halfway up the mountain like a slinky is a narrow

road. "That's where we'll be spending the night.
There's a small village up there that I own."

We hurtled uphill on the stony road. The driver
didn't slow down when we reach the hairpin curves
and Matt swayed this way and that. It was hard to
get changed with all the wild careening. My
stomach was in knots and Lisa kept screaming. I
could tell that Dad was getting impatient with her.
Finally we screeched to a halt. We were on a terrace.
The coca plantations zigzagged all the way down to
the sea of jungle. There was a road of interlocking
stones, straight as an arrow, threading down the
mountain from where we stood, but it wasn't wide
enough for the limousines.

I looked at Dad questioningly. *"El Camino Real,"*
he said, "the Royal Road of the High Incas." We got
out of the limo. The others were climbing out too. I
saw the old woman. Dr. von Steinberg was fanning
himself and Señor Ortega was striding around with
his kid skulking behind. Even though the sun was
beating down on us it was chilly and hard to breathe
because of the altitude.

There was music being played on *rondador* and
quena and *pincilla* — our chauffeur explained all the
different kinds of flutes to us, and a *yaraví* singer
squawking away in Quechua with his big hat
bobbing in the wind.

On one side of the terrace stood a rococo church
with twisting stone columns and gargoyles. Bells
were ringing. There were market stalls thrown up
with wooden crosspieces and awnings of clear blue

plastic. In some of the stalls there were big vats of coca leaves which were being steeped in benzine to release the cocaine. The benzine really stank up the air. It got inside all the other smells, the mutton grilling in garlic and lemon, the heaps of fruit, the llama shit steaming in the cold.

Then there were like these men in gray sheepskin robes wearing headdresses with red feathers — about ten of them — standing in a circle and walking slowly around to the beat of a drum. Matt stopped to stare at them and Señor Ortega was all, "They're rehearsing for *Inti Raymi* , the Sun Festival."

There were also like these guys sitting around a big wooden vat, and they were chewing on sheaves of grain and spitting them out into the vat. The PIP guy told me, with a chuckle, "Oh, they making *chicha* — Inca beer — very strong."

So we trooped into the church and we stood in the antechapel during the elevation of the host. There were these old guys squatting on rugs selling miniature cars and television sets and appliances and houses — you could fit two or three of them in the palm of your hand — all made of sugar. They were taking money right there in the antechapel. Clouds of incense everywhere, almost choking you, but underneath it all there was still the stench of benzine.

When the PIP man comes in with his weapon slung over his shoulder people move aside. There's a bunch of dudes in a different uniform and they look at him nervously until flashes a thumbs-up sign to them. I figure they're members of the Shining Path, which is a guerilla militia we sometimes employ to help out in the business.

Señor Ortega comes up to me and puts his arm over my shoulder. "Is there anything you have ever wished for, Antonio? Car, house," — leering now — "girl friend?" He points to the sugar miniatures. "Anything you want, take." He waves a 500 *inti*-note at the peasant. I kneel down and I select a bunch of stuff — a Porsche, a blonde woman in a bikini — and I get a couple of things for Matt. Matt tries to eat one of them but Señor Ortega stops him. He tells me and Matt to follow him. Juanito shows up behind us and he has his hands full — little TV sets, a couple of houses, sheep, a Mercedes and a Ferrari.

We genuflect as we go into the nave and then he leads us to a side chapel that's twice as crowded as the chapel, plus there's a long line to get it. Women are muttering and crossing themselves and rocking. When we finally reach the altar railing there's a smell like caramel and I see that the people in front of me are tossing their sugar goodies into a brazier in front of the image of the Virgin.

"Go on, children," says Señor Ortega. "Is for Pacha Mama, mother of the earth. The Pope has made her into Mother Mary, but we know better, no?"

He throws his handful into the flames. I watch them shrivel and melt and catch another whiff of caramel. All of his offerings are miniature people. Maybe I'm imagining it but they look like me and Dad and Matt ... one minute they're there ... the next they're charred beyond recognition. I'm staring at the Virgin because you know who it looks like? It looks like the old Indian woman only rejuvenated — and when I look into the eyes of the plaster image they glitter and I hear a voice, *Mi hijo, mi hijo.*

I'm all, "Who said that?" because I see the old woman out of the corner of my eye and then she's gone. She can slip in and out of dark corners like a jaguar in the heart of the jungle. Jesus it makes me nervous.

I toss in my offerings. But when I try to help Matt with his, I miss and his sugar dolls clatter against the side of the brazier. I'm all, "Sorry, Matt," and try to cheer him, but he's gone totally glassy-eyed. I guess Lisa must have thorazined him behind my back.

Juanito does his offering, diffidently avoiding my eyes. It's like they all know something that I don't know. Even Matt seems to know.

Later Señor Ortega left us kids in the line to take communion and went off somewhere. Where were Dad and Lisa? They seemed to all have given us the slip. I'm all, *Fuck* this. I looked for Ortega and I saw him whispering with the old Indian woman. I decided to follow them. The incense was so thick it was hard for them to notice me as I crept right up to them.

I hid behind a column. They went through an archway. I waited for a second. There were side chapels along the colonnade. One to Santa Barbara, which was packed with votive candles and Indians on their hands and knees and like all these decapitated human heads they were offering up, *papier mâché* I guess — and I remembered Dad telling me once that Santa Barbara is really Xangó, a hanged god from somewhere in Africa. I moved on quickly — it gave me the creeps. I passed some empty chapels with more conventional saints like you'd see in Chicago, but they had no one worshipping them.

The organ was booming away as people were taking the host. But I could hear another music too. Coming from somewhere behind the altar.   I followed the colonnade around and the music grew louder. It was a singsongy flute music, Chinese-sounding. There was a stairwell leading downward, I guess into the crypt. The alien music grew louder. My footsteps echoed.

It was freezing down there. I saw marble tombs, the kind that show the body lying in state on top and the rotting skeleton underneath. There were real bones too, arranged in geometric patterns along stone troughs … it made me think of death, though I was   young.   Latin   inscriptions   everywhere. Flickering candlelight. And hushed voices. I inched my way down. The music welled up.

I hid behind one of the tombs. My head was level with the sculpted skull of some sixteenth century hidalgo with a white worm wriggling out of his socket. The marble was cold and damp. I saw a forest of statuary ... gods and goddess, nymphs and shepherds, skeletons and demons ... a marble death with a marble scythe ... among the stone faces there were humans. I saw the old Indian woman. She was naked and spread-eagled against a white sarcophagus. There was a man with his back to me wearing a great embroidered cloak like the one they made we wear in Barranca. He was fucking the woman. Wildly pumping away I mean, and she was thrusting in time to the fluting of three blind musicians. Fucking in church. This wasn't like tagging the L-train, this was a *mortal* sin. Jesus I was shocked. I didn't know what to do. I crossed myself. Not that I'm religious. This was beyond religion. I crossed myself two more times. "Mother of God," I said.

Other people were watching intently: Dr. von Steinberg ... Ortega ... de la Verdad ... Knightley. Whispering to each other. Nudging and winking.

The man in the cloak pulled away from the woman and turned around and I realized that it was my father.

I crept closer.

The Indian woman's face ... was it the incense? ... it was less shriveled somehow ... she seemed younger.

My father was saying, "I don't want to go through with it."

The old woman said, "You think it is what I want, *mi señor?* I am the giver of life."

My father said, "This is the 1990s, my friends. The world has changed."

"We all have these feelings, *compadre,*" said Ortega. "But the world has not changed. Everything is as it always will be, *saecula saeculorum.*"

Then this man in a Shining Path uniform comes charging down the stairs. I duck behind a pillar. He's got a baton with cords dangling from it, and he's bleeding and he has one eye swollen shut. He hands the *quipu* to my father. Dad scans the knotted ropes — I'm amazed he can read them and even more at what he says next: "This is the end," he says. "I can't go on. We can't continue in business without the Panquechochac fields. I'm going to take my kids and go back home ... maybe even turn myself in. There's only so much *compadrazgo* I can deal with. I'm not like you."

I've never seen him look so defeated. My Dad's not the kind of guy who ever gives up.

"*Ay, mierditas!*" says Ortega.

The Indian woman says, "You are the chosen one. You have ploughed the earth and you must seed the sky. It is time."

At that moment there's an earsplitting crack. Several of the statues crash to the floor. The pillar buckles and Dad sees me.

"Tony!" he screams. "What are you —"

The whole church is shaking.   Everyone's screaming all at once. We have to get out. I run for the steps. I don't know if it's an earthquake or what but I think I'm going to piss myself. I don't think about it, I just sprint up those coiling steps, skinning my elbows against the railing. In the nave, people are diving under pews or swarming for the exits. Suddenly I see Matt. He's standing alone, in front of the altar, about to receive communion, only the priest and the altar boys have bolted.

"Matthew!" I shriek at the top of my lungs and I scramble toward him just as the ceiling starts to cave in. I tackle him and we land in the cantoris choir stalls and the flying rubble just misses his head. I look up and I can see the sky through the cracks and I can see helicopter gunships. So it's not an earthquake. It's a fucking *air raid*. And there's a dead woman next to us, sliced in two, sluicing us with gore. I cover Matt's eyes, I bury him under me, I tuck the two of us under the seat and the whole building reverberates and the people's screams are drowned in the roaring … "We gotta get outside, Matt … come on …" The choppers seem fainter now. "We gotta make a run for it."

We scramble out from under pew. I'm holding a leather bible over our heads. The fan vaulting overhead is shattered and the sunlight streams down. There's a gash in the wall and we dash for it and we find ourselves out there in the plaza where things are going crazy. People are taking cover under market stalls, under oxcarts, behind our limos. People are streaming downhill … a ribbon of human flesh twisting and turning across terraces of coca. Benzine vats are on fire. A woman is on fire and rolling across the *Camino,* trying to put herself out. Her shriek is like the wail of the Andean flute. I hold onto Matt's hand. He stands there stock still like a dead kid with unseeing eyes … *fuck* Lisa for doping him up this much, *fuck fuck fuck.*

"Dad!" There he is. At the very edge of the precipice. He's standing there with all his cronies. The Indian woman is there too and she has on a headdress of feathers and she has a cloak over her naked body that flaps in the wind like the plastic awnings in the market stalls like the bloodstained blankets hanging up for sale. "Come on Matt. Come on, Dad's there." I have to tug hard to get him to move. The choppers make another pass and fire leaps rat-tat-tat from stall to stall. I have to drag Matt across piles of brick, across a child's charred body. The Shining Path guys are firing at the sky with their anti-aircraft weapons. There's smoke everywhere. It's in my eyes down my throat and I'm suffocating. But I have to get Matt to safety. I'm exhausted as I reach the edge of the terrace. A herd of alpaca scatters across the paving, The ground never stops shaking.

My Dad looks out over the great green steps toward the distant jungle. The farthest fields are already on fire. Fire is climbing the massive green steps that contain our family's wealth. Black smoke roils across the horizon. The smell of greenwood burning mingles with the porkfat stink of sizzling people. Dad seems so distant from it all and so unreachable.

The Indian woman says: "You see how it must be, Rodolfo Severini. The universe is one of cause and effect. The true forces do not forgive like white men's gods. A bargain was struck in heaven as it was on earth."

My father can't find the words to answer her. It's Señor Ortega who brushes her aside and says, "Do not flagellate him, *bruja!* You enjoy his pain too much. The thing we do is sacred."

"We have celebrated the sacred union of earth and sky, and I have brought forth fruit!" the woman says. "The world must be renewed!" And she begins to weep. Her change of mood is sudden and total.

"I must," Dad says. "I have no choice. This is what I chose. This is the bargain I sealed, twenty years ago."

At last he seemed to see me and Matt. And Juanito too, snivelling as he stepped forward from a cloud of smoke. The church explodes.

"Get ready, kids. We have to go up the mountain."

I looked at the others and saw they were like heaving sighs of relief. This was something they'd all been waiting for and dreading, I guess.

I knew he had come to a terrible decision and he was trying to bury his pain deep inside himself the way a man should. I would have done anything to make the hurt go away, but I knew, when he made up his mind like this, that nothing in the world could change it. The last time I saw his face darken like this was when he had to order a hit on Uncle Eduardo after he narked to the FBI. Eduardo was Dad's favorite brother.

   ***

The battle is still raging when we start up the mountain — me and my Dad and Matt and Lisa and the Ortegas and Dr. von Steinberg and several others. At first the journey is by Land Rover and is not so bad. More hairpin curves, but once you got used to the rhythm, the swing, it was no worse than an upside-down roller coaster, over and over and over.

Halfway again, just before the snow line, the road petered out and there was a *tambo*, a resting spot for messengers of the High Inca. It was a stone hut refurbished for us with a Primus stove and some canned food. There were people waiting for us with about a dozen llamas laden with sacks and mountain-climbing gear. The people were all pureblooded Indians, I think: none of them could speak a world of Spanish. They wore red ponchos and headdresses with feathers and some of them had gold ornaments in their earlobes, like the bolts in Frankenstein's head. Dad greeted them with, *"Napaykullayki!"*

When they saw us they began whispering among themselves and I heard the word *capacocha* many times.

"They've been waiting for thirteen years for this moment, son," my father said.

We stood on a ledge. I peered down over the sheer rock. The mountains around us weren't all jagged like the Rockies but were like curved, like bells or flasks. It was pretty up here and you could barely see the air raid going on, and the choppers were all tiny like dragonflies. It was cold — God was it cold. I was wearing a couple of blankets over my winter clothes and if the air was thin down there in the village here it seemed like a fucking vacuum. My face was all numb and Matt was worse off than me, he was doped to the gills. Even when I closed my eyes and concentrated real hard I couldn't hear him inside my head like I usually can, and even if there'd been a still small voice there it would've been slaughtered by the way the wind was screeching and roaring.

I'm all standing there with Dad and I try to outshout the wind: "Dad," I'm all, "Dad, what are you into here? What kind of bargain did you make with these dudes? ... what were you doing to that woman in church, I mean like, we *are* Catholic, aren't we?"

Dad says: "It's all the same religion underneath, son." And then he says, "I love you."

"I love you too, Dad ... but I don't understand."

"Have you ever dreamed of being king of the sky, lord of the wind, dreamer of the world's dreams?"

"No, Dad."

I realized that this was the question Ortega had asked me before. The question Matt asked me in my dream. It made me scared. I didn't know why but I wanted to just run off that mountain and leap back into my bed in Chicago and wake up and tell myself it was all inside my head.

We went back to the stone hut. We spread our sleeping bags out on a granite floor piled high with rugs. Sometimes you could still hear the choppers. The wind shrilled and I tossed and turned and dreamed about the dead kid sitting in his plastic *huaca* in Chicago. Matt didn't appear to me that night. I think the part of him that comes to me in dreams had shriveled up and collapsed in on itself. Because of the cold. Jesus, the cold.

I lay there and played Tetris on my gameboy by flashlight. Everyone else slept soundly. But Dad sat up all night, I think. On a big old throne hewn out of rock. The Indians called it an *unsu,* a seat of the gods.

***

Climbing the mountain: after a while you forget there's a whole world outside the domain of the *apu,* the mountain spirit. There's the cold of course. It's a seeping cold. You think you've gone numb and you can't feel anything on your skin but that's when it's already gone all the way into your bones and every

inch is agony. You wonder how anyone could ever
have done this before. But you know it's been done
because every step of the way is clearly marked.
There are steps beneath the ice, chiseled from naked
rock, and here and there markers and petroglyphs
with leering faces peering from the snow. Your feet
are blocks of ice and you just go on trudging,
trudging, taking the pain. There's snow on
everything. On top of the llamas' packs. I'm
wearing three alpaca sweaters under my sheepskin
and it doesn't make a dent in the cold. And then
there's not being able to breathe. Now and then we
stop for oxygen — we're carrying a tank of it on a
llama's back — but the Indians never need it, they
just go tramping upward to the sky.

And this was the easy part of the slope. We
climbed from dawn until sunset. We didn't talk
because of the wind. Porfirio Knightley liked to beat
the llamas with a cudgel, but it didn't make them
move any faster.

There was another *tambo* where we spent another
restless night. It was that night that Matt came to
me once more in my dreams. We were skating
together, side by side, down an endless sewage
tunnel. There was graffiti everywhere but like I
didn't recognize any of the taggers' names. You
could hear the far shriek of the wind beyond, not the
windy city's wind but the thin and desolate wind of
the Andes. We skated swiftly with our trucks
perfectly greased and our knees and hips swaying in

perfect time almost like we were one kid alone in the long dark tunnel.

We didn't talk for a long time. I was happy. This was the summer I wanted to have.

"I'm sorry it has to end, Tony," Matt says. "But I'm not afraid anymore."

We skate down the long tunnel toward darkness.

"What do you mean, Matt?"

We link up, arms across shoulders, as we give ourselves to the rhythm of the skateboard, whoosh, bend, whoosh, bend.

I'm all, "Why does it have to end?"

"You're gonna betray me, Tony. But it's okay. The *ayllu* comes first."

"I don't even know what an *ayllu* is. You've lost me." His fingers, on my shoulders, are cold as steel, and bony, as we go skating to darkness down the long tunnel.

"The *ayllu* is the family. You and me and Dad and our mother … and the community … and the nation … and the earth."

"Our mother?"

And then I hear the voice of the Indian woman, saying *mi hijo, mi hijo.* And I know what it means.

—*mi hijo mi hijo mi hijo*—

And when I wake up I see the Indian woman's face, bending over mine, looking at me in the flickering light of a parafin lamp. Matt is asleep. He hasn't reallu woken up since we started up the mountain. And there's Dad, on his *unsu*, draped in crimson blankets. The Indian woman isn't old at all.

Her old age was just an optical illusion, I guess. The wind is howling but there's warmth in the stone room, warmth that comes from her. Her face is shining. It's how you always imagine the Blessed Virgin might look when they teach you about the Assumption in catechism. You can almost hear the choir singing far away even though you know it's just the wind.

"Are you my mother?" I ask her.

She says, *"Wawachay, wawachay."* I think it means *my son.* Then she goes into a corner and the light fades and the warmth with it. I go to my Dad, who's sitting on his throne.

"Dad?"

He looks up at me. And he's all old — *old!* — like he's sucked up all the family troubles into himself. So I say to him, "You told me that all religions are like, the same underneath, right? And you made some kind of bargain with these people where you had to boff the old *strega* so the natives would like think you were their king, am I right? And now this thing has gone too far somehow. But what's to stop us from saying *basta* already? Stop the world so we can get off?"

"It's not as simple as it looks, son," Dad says. He's wheezing like an old man. "Listen, I'll tell you a bedtime story. Come here."

I can hardly squeeze onto his lap anymore but I feel that he really needs me to be like a little kid again. So I put my arms around him and I lean my head against his neck. His five o'clock shadow prickles my forehead and I laugh a little, and then he says, "All religions are the same underneath, so I'll tell you a folk tale from Southeast Asia. It's about Prince Vessandar, who was the ninth avatar of the god Vishnu. He was a great a powerful prince who ruled over the richest kingdom in the world. But even in this kingdom there was poverty and homelessness. People eating out of trashcans and warming themselves over grates in the middle of winter. Are you listening, Tony?"

"Uh huh." I'm drifting. I can see Matt stir a little in his sleep. I can see the old Inca woman standing with her palms folded, with her blankets billowing around her, bathed in soft light.

"Prince Vessandar vowed to give away everything he had. It didn't matter who came to his door or what they asked for. Finally he became a hermit and he went with his two small sons to live in a dark forest at the foot of the Himalayas.

"One day a wicked man named Chuchok came to the forest. He was greedy. His wife wanted to have slaves, because she was too lazy to do anything around the house. So he went to Vessandar's cave and said, 'I've heard that you're the idiot madman who sits in a a cave all day and gives away all his possessions to anyone who asks. I dare you! Give me your children to be my slaves. I will abuse them and I will mistreat them. You have to give them to me or you'll be untrue to your vow.'

"So Prince Vessandar said, 'Take them.' And he sent the children down from the cave."

"What a fuckhead," I said sleepily.   "What a terrible father."

My father hugged me tight and he kissed me on the cheek and I tasted something salt.   This time I really knew he was weeping. And he said, "No, no, you see, he loved his children more than anything in the world. The story is not meant to teach you not to love your children.   But in the moment that he gave them up, he understood that everything in the universe is transient. He was filled with compassion for all living things. In his next life he would return to earth as the Buddha.   And you see, the evil Chuchok was punished and the children were rescued, so it all came out all right in the end. I suppose I could have told you the story of Abraham and Isaac, too, but you had that in catechism."

I understood it all then.   He had told me all about it that day at the field museum. *They left him in a temple on a mountain in the Andes. Offered him to Wiraqocha, creator of the universe. That's how the High Inca kept the empire together — with treaties between himself and all the subsidiary kingdoms, sealed by the mutual exchange of children for sacrifice.* The business was failing. The PIP and probably the Americans were burning down the coca fields.   Dr. von Steinberg had examined me and found me to be without blemish. Oh, there was the mole, but he'd burned it off, so how were the gods to know? In the dream, Matt got it all wrong. He didn't had to take a physical — just me, the *capacocha,* the sacrifice.

"You're going to fucking kill me, Dad," I said. "It's for the good of the *ayllu* and all shit, but it doesn't make it any easier to take. I mean, Jesus Christ, my own father."

"I tried everything, son," he said.

It is the strangest moment I've ever had in my relationship with my Dad. I feel so fucking close to him I almost don't mind dying. That's how much I understand what he's going through. The Indians being gunned down from the sky, the fields on fire, the church getting blown to kingdom come. Oh Jesus, he's in agony. He feels responsible for it somehow and he thinks my death is the only solution. It's what I was born for. It's my destiny.

My father dries his tears on the alpaca blanket. I don't cry because I can't really grasp it all. It's so cosmic and yet it's as personal as the love we feel for each other, me and him. And so we fall asleep like this, huddled together, secure against the whole world.

***

Then came the hardest part of the climb. We had to leave the pack animals behind. We crossed a mile-deep ravine on a rope bridge. The world was white. It burned our eyes. Then there were steps, step after slippery step. On the easier stretches they carried us — me and Matt and Dad and Lisa in litters made of woven rushes. Toward the end the footholds were far between and the Indians hauled us up in baskets. I remember dangling, with the wind smashing me against the ice wall over and over, not feeling the pain or the cold.

At the peak of the mountain there was a temple. Staircases led nowhere. There were walls of gigantic interlocking stones half-buried in the snow. There were stone shelters linked by passageways hollowed out of the mountain. Caverns within caverns. We all made for the first shelter. The Indians broke out the *chuñu* — which is like freeze-dried potatoes and gross-tasting — and some guinea pigs and started a fire to roast them in, and a few of them sat around in a circle and passed around a handful of coca leaves. They didn't seem at all fazed by the fact that they were going to kill me.

"Damn *huaqueros* have been here," Señor Ortega said ruefully. There were tools lying around. Someone had tried to pry away stones from the wall. "Damn *huaqueros*, they come here with their foundation grants and their shovels, and they write their dissertations, and they rob us blind."

"They steal away even our gods," said Señor Knightley.

It had been squalling a moment before we reached the summit, but here there was no wind at all. The temple was like in its own space, separate from the rest of the world. Looking out through the chinks in the wall, I could see for miles and miles. I could see mountain upon mountain, but our mountain was the king of them all. I could see past the mountains; I could see the jungle and the desert and the sea. I don't know if I really saw all this or if it was just with my inner eye. But I know I felt I was king of it all, like I grasped the cosmos in my hand like a baseball. If I only yawned, the wind would spring from my lips and whirl across the land. If I cried then rain would stream down from the sky and if I laughed the thunder would shake the rooftops of Cuzco and even of Schaumburg and Barrington. For a tiny moment I wanted to be king of the sky.

The grownups all went away to be robed. Me and Matt were left alone in the room. The guinea-pigs were searing on hot stones and their smoke swirled around us.

"This is it, brother," I said to him. "No more scamming chicks or tagging the L-train."

Matt looked into my eyes for a long time. For a moment I thought, Shit, he's going to speak, I'm drifting into a dream. But no. I was wide awake.

Then they came to take me to the holy place.

It's just like the one at the Field Museum. Except the walls aren't concrete. They're solid stone and caked with ice. The floor is a sheet of ice. Our breath hangs in the air. There is no wind here. There's an utter stillness. You feel you're profaning just by being there. I've never felt like this, not even in confession.

"Damn *huaqueros!*" Señor Ortega says again. And then I see what he means. There is a raised *unsu* dead center in the room. But there's no dead kid and no pile of offerings. Just an empty packet of Winstons and a crumpled can of Budweiser. They've taken everything of value. How could they not feel daunted by the spirit of this place? Jesus, I fucking feel it in my bones, in my soul.

The porters have come in now. They're looking sheepishly at me as they lay down gifts in front of the *unsu*. They're the offerings that were given to me back in Lima: the bundles of 10,000 *inti* notes, the television, baskets of food and jugs of *chicha*, the Game Boy I've been playing with since our road trip started.

"Is that why your fields are being wasted by chopper fire and your people are being driven into poverty and homelessness?" I say. "Is it because someone ripped off your god? Because he's sitting behind a plexiglass window in a museum in downtown Chicago?"

No one will look me in the eye. I've become *huaca*, a sacred thing.

My father stands beside the *unsu* with his robes and feathers and glittering ornaments. He's as old as the whole world. Next to him is the woman, who is Pacha Mama, the earth goddess, who is my mother, who is the Blessed Virgin. Jesus she's beautiful. She's like a painting above a church altar. Matt is there too, all bundled up, looking frail and disconsolate. I haven't heard him, not in my dreams and not in my head, since the dream with the long dark tunnel.

I hear the mountain calling me and I'm thinking how good it will feel to sit up here forever and be king of the sky and ruler of the wind....

Dr. von Steinberg comes into the chamber. He has a silver platter in his hands and on it there are gold funerary gloves. Just my size.

Porfirio Knightley comes in wearing a sun-disk on his head, draped in a red cloak. Lisa comes in with a tray of hypodermic syringes. They're not going to let me feel any pain. I'm going to go out little by little, like a votive candle.

They start to chant in Quechua. Their voices are hypnotic and I feel myself drifting into the land of dreams, I feel myself skating down the tunnel. But I'm alone and the tunnel has no exit. I'm skating, down, down, down. Their voices drone on. There's no heat in the cave but I don't feel cold anymore. They go on chanting by the light of a thousand candles, and now and then they scatter incense that clogs my nostrils and dulls my thoughts. I can feel them taking my clothes away and painting my face and covering me with cold gold ornaments. I can feel their hands in mine as they lead me toward the sacred throne.

My father says to me: "Do you wish to become king of the sky?"

I look up at him. No one sees us gazing in each other's eyes. No one sees the thoughts we exchange. They're all standing with their eyes averted. There's a flash of understanding. I see with total clarity what has to be done. Because we are both kings. Jesus, I think, all this time he's been hoping against hope that I'll be able to read his mind, because the words that must be said can only be said by me.

I say, "You can't sacrifice me against my will. Isn't that why each of you has been asking me if I wish to become king of the sky? If I say *yes* then I say the word of power that sets the whole thing in motion. I have the power to withhold everything. All I have to do is say *no*. And that's what I'm saying. No."

They're all staring at me now. There's shock in their faces. I guess this hasn't happened in five hundred years.

I go on, "There's only one practical solution. If Dad dies, who will be your king? How can a mute person rule a *ayllu* of a thousand *ayllukuna*? You have to sacrifice Matt, not me. It was ordained."

I hate myself for saying this. But I know now why Matt is here. I know why Dad has hauled him along with us all this way. I know Dad loves Matt as much as he loves me. I know I love Matt more than anyone in the world. But I have to give him up. For the sake of the *ayllu*. "Examine him, Dr. von Steinberg," I say. "He doesn't have any blemishes. Not even a mole on the shoulder like the one you scraped away."

Matt has gone rigid. It's like he already feels the cold steal over him, seep into him, turn him to stone.

"But," my father says, "how do we know that he is willing?"

I close my eyes. I call to him in the kingdom of my dreams. I know he's there, afraid, hiding. I can feel him. In my mind I cry out to him: Matt, say yes, say yes … I know he won't say it. I know how scared he is of death. I search for him in the tunnel of darkness but he's smeared himself along the walls among the graffiti so I won't be able to find him. I can feel him resisting me. Inside the freezing boy with the icy eyes there's a boy full of rage who cannot speak, cannot defend himself, and I have to speak for him. And so I lie, with passion in my voice to hide my deception: "He's willing. I've read it in his mind. He wants to become king of the sky and ruler of the wind. He is the real *capacocha*."

And I am the only one who feels the force of his anger. And I am the only one who knows I have betrayed the person who most trusted me.

That is how to be a king.

So they took the gold neckpiece off me and put it around Matt's neck. They fitted him with the funerary gloves and the anklets and the armbands of gold. Matt stood there like a Ken doll, letting them put the vestments on him, letting them lead him to the *unsu*. Lisa pumped him full of morphine and demerol. The offerings were laid at his feet and the Indians prostrated themselves and would not look in his face. And me, I felt the numbness leave me. I felt the cold in my joints and the tears freezing against my cheeks. When I could feel pain again I knew that I wasn't going to die.

They crossed his legs and folded his gold-cased hands into position. And I went up to him to kiss him goodbye. He was already as hard and cold as the mountain granite. But in the moment that my lips brushed his cheek, I saw him look at me with hurt and with total, unconscionable hatred. And then his eyes went dead.

***

Summer's ending and I'm going into the ninth grade. When we came back from Peru the FBI arrested my Dad. They charged him with some kind of bullshit and our pictures were in the *Enquirer* and so I guess it's the end of public school for me.

I skated the whole summer long with my friends and came this close to losing my virginity along with my innocence.

I still talk to Matt in my dreams sometimes. But we're drifting apart. He has a world to watch over and I still have all those kid things to work through. We don't have much in common anymore. I'll always be haunted by my betrayal of him. Matt's a god now so maybe he'll forgive me, but I don't know if I can forgive myself. Yet it had to be done. And it's brought me and Dad a lot closer. We talk about everything now. He's the best dad in the whole world. Shit, I love him more now than in the old days, because I have to love him enough for me *and* Matt now.

I'm sure Dad will be back in business by next week. He'll never spend a day in jail, because we have the gods on our side. The FBI can't fight my brother, the silent one, the wind from the highest peak.

In the Andes there are gods all over the mountains. The gods are children — the most powerless of humans — who have been translated through death into the most powerful beings in the world. I guess that's only fair. It's good to know there's a god up there who has the same blood as me, who will always be my brother.

I'm looking forward to having Juanito here next summer. I miss having Matt around. It'd be good to have like a younger brother. I want to teach him how to do a perfect 360° and how to scam with Chicago chicks. It'll be rad.

They better lay off the cocaine trade real soon. If they keep burning our crops I'll end up losing Juanito before I've even had a chance to know him. That'd suck. There aren't any mountains around here anyway, so we'd probably have to like buy a penthouse in the Sears tower and install an apartment size deep freeze. I guess those are the kinds of decisions I'm going to have to make one day.

It's hard to be a ruler of men, harder than you'll ever know.

— Sun Valley, California, 1988

FIRE FROM THE WINE-DARK SEA

This story, written in 1979, was my first fantasy story. I had published no novels as yet, only a number of science fiction short stories, mostly set in the "Inquestor" and "Mallworld" universes, when Roy Torgeson, editing an anthology series called Other Worlds *for Zebra Books, asked me to see if I could come up with a fantasy story. It had not, until that moment, ever occurred to me that I would write fantasy ... or that I would eventually be perceived more as a dark fantasist than a writer of science fiction.*

The real life roots of the story are as follows: I have a close friend named Deborah, who has two sons, twins, who are much like the two boys in my short story. They do — or did at that time — spend their summers in a small seaside town in Massachussets. Deborah was, and is, a fine pianist as well as a woman whose maternal abilities would put June Cleaver to shame; and her family was, and is, charmingly and refreshingly foulmouthed. The sons have done well. One has had his picture in Time *magazine, an honor which has yet to fall to me. (I was once interviewed for* People, *but the week in which the story was slated to appear was the one when Michael Jackson's hair caught on fire. I was squeezed out, never to reemerge.)*

Beethoven's Opus 111 piano sonata, it has been said, encompasses the twin polarities of sansara *and* nirvana. *If you can, listen to the second movement while reading this story. If you listen carefully, it shouldn't even be necessary to read the story....*

Κι αν πτωχική την βρεις, η Ιθάκη
δεν σε γέλασε. Έτσι σοφός που έγινες, μετόση
πείρα, ήδη θα το κατάλαβες η Ιθάκες τι σημαίνουν.

And if when you finally reach Ithaca, you find her poor,
It is not because Ithaca has deceived you. Rather,
You have become so much wiser, so much more experienced,
That you will already have understood what these Ithacas mean.

        — Kavafis

Fire from the Wine-Dark Sea

Once upon a time there was a man who had two sons, twins; they had wild wheatfield hair that rustled in rough winds and was bleached still whiter in summer, and pale freckles, and snub noses, and smiles that burst out, crooked teeth and all, like sunlight after a stormfall, and great dark darting daunting eyes.

People would stare at them, searching for a difference, and they usually couldn't find one. They also stared because they were shockingly beautiful kids. Of course the man could tell the difference; he was their father.

For the man, what was difficult was another thing — having two such beautiful children, and knowing that he loved one of them better…

I've started this all wrong, haven't I? When you've got the Poetry Chair at some obscure New England university, you feel, an obligation to talk this way, to write this way; it's the literary syndrome.

Because words are in themselves beautiful things ..
Like gems. Like clothes. Like coffins. Hiding the
hurt.

Well. Shit.

You see, this man I'm writing about. It's no fairy
tale. It's not; an archetypal hypothetical mythopoeic
paradigm out there in a house by the sea, scribbling
ironic Byronic laconic verses into a tattered
notebook. Maybe this man exists, but the man in this
story isn't him.

He's me.

So I think I'll desist from this "universalizing"
crap now. I only began that way because it's so scary,
trying to write about: something real. something that
happened. You want to escape into "he did this," "he
did that." And yet....

It's because of this very story that I don't ever
want to run away from anything again.

First person.

Summers we lived by the sea, in our estate two
miles down from the village of St. Joan—it's
pronounced "Sin-jun"— in an old house ghosted
with grandfathers, on Delenda Circle that curved off
Moore Avenue that ran from the village and route
311, past Charley's Cliffs and along the Cape for
many miles. From my window and from the boys'
window you saw the sea mostly, a ribbon of beach at
high tide, and a fuzzy Tuckatinck Island, white and
gray-green.

Mornings Sandy and Claude would go running
before I woke, up the avenue a bit and then into

DuPertuis Lane, twistier than a cat-pawed yarn ball
and smelling of old earth and moss, and tall woods
peering over the mist...

One morning I was meditating on the sunny side
of an egg when Sandy burst through the kitchen
door. Everything always exploded from silent black-
and-white to technicolor sensurround whenever he
came into a room..., "Harry!" he yelled. "Harry!
We've found a friend!"

"Who —?"

"Coming up behind us! Running behind, up
DuPertuis Lane, rounding the corner... C'mon,
Harold, Mr. Vance, come see!"

He stopped for a breath. Christ, what a kid! With
a grandly unselfconscious movement he swept back
his hair. It remained a mess, moss-sprinkled and
mussed by the morning wind. Then he shucked his
sneakers over the table. They arced over the eggs
and crashed on the stoneware tiles, and he smiled a
little.

"Sandy, who is he?" I said.

"We don't know, Harry."

Then Claude stood quietly in the doorway, his
face gridded by the screen, and the sunrise sparking
darts through his hair.

The room temperature seemed to drop a notch.

"Hi, Dad."

It's funny, how Sandy never called me that.
Always — with a wryness concealing awkward
tenderness — 'Harold,' or 'Harry,' or 'Mr Vance.'

Kids that age hate to give anything away ... and yet it was Sandy I loved the most, wild Sandy.

"Sandy—" I touched him but he slipped through my fingers like sea spray. Claude said, "Dad, he's very strange, the man. I don't know if I like him. He keeps babbling on about...oh, weird stuff."

"He's terrific!" Sandy said.

"Yah," said Claude, coming in and pressing against the door hinges to make them squeak. He came and sat down at the kitchen table. He moved unsteadily, the way a thirteen-year-old usually does; he was different in this from Sandy, who moved with his Whole being, elemental, like a wild animal. He took off his sneakers very carefully and put them down on either side of a tile crack, so that it would be a completely symmetrical pattern.

I watched them both for a while. What kind of weirdo had they picked up at the beach or in the woods? I looked from one to the other: Sandy's eyes seemed to trust you so blindly, while Claude's were never innocent, they had a way of shaming you, of putting you in the wrong.

Then I heard a voice form outside. "Phew! These bare feet are no good for running along your roads." It was a rich voice, like someone playing the cello in a marble bathroom...

"Oh, Jesus Christ," I said. "Do you guys have to bring in everyone you meet? Can't a fellow eat his breakfast?"

"But Dad—" said Claude.

"Harry, you'll like him," Sandy said, and I swallowed my exasperation for a second, and then the room went dark because the stranger filled up the doorway completely.

He was tall, fair, with a torn white tunic on, and a trim beard. He was sunburnt. He didn't smile. I looked at him, rather belligerently —

And he transfixed me with his eyes, dark and formidable as my sons' eyes could be sometimes, and cold as a winter wind. And then I noticed that his hair was streaming behind him like fire. But there was no wind in the room at all. I started to say something angry but my mouth was chilled shut ...

Then the coldness melted away and he seemed all friendliness. "These...sneakers, you call them," he said, half-laughing, "a fabulous exotic treasure indeed! Hermes could not be swifter than a stripling shod with these ..." He knelt down to look at Sandy's Adidases, carelessly thrown there on the brown tiles. He picked one of them up and began to poke it, as though he'd never seen one before.

I got my voice back then. "Of all the nerve!" I said. "Marching .. into a stranger's house like this, peering at his things —"

He rose up then, and stared at me very seriously until I felt guilty — the way Claude could always do — and said, "I've come an awful long way." His hair never stopped billowing. "Thousands of miles. Would you turn me out, Mr. Vance? You boys have been most kind to me..."

"Who are you?" I said, more quietly.

"I am," he said, "Odysseus, King of Ithaca."

"See, Dad?" said Claude, laughing suddenly. "I told you he was weird."

"Now look here..." I was desperately scanning the news-, paper in my mind. There had to be some kind of headline like *PSYCHOPATH FLEES EMERGENCY WARD*, something like that. I floundered for something to say, and came out with: "Okay, you're Napoleon — hoops — Odysseus. How come you're not speaking classical Greek, then?"

"I am."

And then I saw it.

When he spoke, it wasn't in lip-synch. I mean what I was hearing didn't synchronize with what his mouth was doing. I mean my God, it was like watching a Godzilla movie. And then there was the hair. And the tunic, too ... lashed by a still tempest.

Now I was really frightened. Claude said, "It's being translated straight into our minds. Like, you know, telepathy, some kind of radar, something—"

But Sandy didn't say anything at all. He seemed just to accept the stranger, to know he was all right, without looking for an explanation.

"I've left Ithaca for good," the stranger said. "After ten years of war, ten years of high adventure, who can stay home? And that Penelope ... so perfect, so patient and everything. Every time I so much as looked at her she would accuse me with her eyes, never meaning to of course, but you just knew she was swallowing her suffering and trying to look beautiful for you. She has her loom now, and I — I wander over the sea, landing in new countries and new epochs, exchanging gifts with the strange new people…"

"Either that, or you're a hell of a good actor," I said. The eggs had grown cold now. "Harry, can he stay here?" Sandy pleaded. "He has to get supplies, and —"

"Well …" I saw that Claude had turned away and was staring at the wall. There was so much eagerness in Sandy's eyes…

"It would please me much, sir, if I could call you my guest-friend," Odysseus said.

I didn't know what to think.

Claude got up suddenly and said: "Dad, I'm going up to the den to use your typewriter." He had this craze for doing concrete poetry, picked up from a whacky creative writing teacher at his school…

I watched my son cross the living room and run up the stairs, his fingers skimming the banister. Not looking at the man, I said, "If only I could believe your story … but it can't be happening. You can't be real."

Odysseus said, "Mr. Vance, you are a poet. You of all people should know how tenuous the line between reality and fantasy is. If the line itself is a fantasy, then fantasy must of necessity be real …"

"You talk like Odysseus should talk." I said. "Wily, word-twisting, devious. You should do well in our century."

It was easy to fall right into what he was saying. He made it sound all so plausible.

"So can he stay, huh, Harry?"

I saw them exchanging a look. He had my son quite hypnotized. Well. that wasn't surprising. And I scrutinized his face. still avoiding his eyes. searching for a trace of deceit. and I couldn't find anything at all ... and the wind on his face never stopped blowing.

I knew his eyes were on me and without meaning to I was raising my eyes to meet his ... they were so dark. Even in the morning light they were crystals of night.

"Wait till you see his ship!" cried Sandy.

Odysseus laughed. "It isn't much of one, judging by the monstrosities I have seen. breasting the tides in the middle of nowhere..."

"He has a ship?" I gasped. "You can see it from the window!" and Sandy had run to the stairs and was springing up them like a cat.

Odysseus said to me. "Beautiful child. Beautiful ... 'sneakers' ... He was holding one of Sandy's, hefting it from hand to hand. And then he smiled a broad sunny smile. and gathered up his tunic more tightly around him. bracing himself against the wind I couldn't feel, and we went up to the boys' room on the second floor.

I could hear Claude tapping laboriously on the typewriter j from my den.

Sandy was gazing out of the window. Without turning. around. he beckoned for me to come and stand by him. I stood over him and he didn't push me away; and I saw a little boat moored on the beach. on our private dock. next to our own boat. Nothing very strange about it ….

"That's it?"

"No. Dad." he said — he never called me that! — and pointed. Out over the sparkle-kissed dark water. to where Tuckatinck Island blocked the horizon. "Don't you see it?" That boat's only his little shuttle."

I couldn't see anything at first. "What do you mean. Sandy?"

And then I saw a vague white outline. as though a cloud had settled on the distant shoreline. Perhaps a mast. Perhaps a sail. Perhaps a prow chiselled into a nude woman with wide-open arms. I couldn't tell…"

"See, Harry?" He was yelling excitedly. "There are people walking the decks, the sails are flapping…"

"Damn it, I don't see anything! I guess you just have better eyesight than me."

"You suck shit, Mr. Vance!" he said, childish suddenly.

I shrugged. "I guess your peculiar friend will be with us for a few days, huh?" I looked at the man expectantly. Then I turned around and tried to turn the cloud that hugged the island into a firm-outlined ship, with planks, masts, rivets, but the haze would not resolve…"

"Just long enough to look around," said Odysseus. "Already I long for the sea, for tastier adventures. But I'd like to take something with me, a souvenir perhaps … at every port I take some gift from the inhabitants. After all, I am a King."

He and Sandy exchanged a look.

In that moment I knew that I was jealous.

"Sure," I said.

Claude's typing pelted the silence.

***

Claude woke me up by putting on one of Laura's records. The one of Beethoven's last piano sonata, the opus one one one, with the long impossible trills that seem to stretch from your guts to the end of the sky. Laura had played it at her last concert.

(Laughing Laura! The arms like wild cranes in flight. Sweeping up from the keyboard like Sandy springing from the diving rock by Charley's Cliffs. Laughing alone in the Albert Hall before the audience came on, confounding the ushers. Darting from the underground at Piccadilly Circus. Stepping in front of a double decker bus.)

"Dad...?"

(Coming back to the States. Clearing the coffin through customs.)

Claude: a slim shadow crossing the bed, bisecting the triangle of dawn light from the half-closed shutters.

(Really? Four years ago?)

"Dad..."

I felt a pang of guilt, suddenly. I couldn't think why, except that I'd neglected the kid, as always. "Hey, why aren't you out running with Sandy, Claudius?"

"He took Odysseus with him." Then — the anguish in his voice all out of proportion with what he was saying — "Dad, he lent him *your* sneakers!"

I suppressed the unreasonable, un-adult annoyance I felt.

"Besides," he said, "I hate to run. I only do it to be with him."

"And now—"

"He's with the immortal stranger."

— the piano had reached the first of the long trills —

"Daddy, I think he's surrounded by some kind of time-shield, you know, like a force field. It keeps him locked away from our universe, you know. And we don't know what he's really saying either. It's all dubbed, but the translation could be wrong, you know like in Swedish movies when they're really saying 'oh, fuck,' or something, and it comes out 'jeepers.' Or he's come bursting through from an alternate universe—"

"Yeah."

I didn't really know what he was saying; you know faculty kids. Smart as hell, old before their time. Smartass, too. He was hiding something though, under the froth of words. I said, as gently as I could, "What's up, kid?"

He sat down on the bed then. I could feel him against my knee, and I could feel the tension between us like a jack-in-the box ready to burst. "You love him a lot, don't you, Dad?" he said. "More than me."

I was silent.

"That's all right, Dad. I want you to know that. I do too." He was talking at the shutters, trying not to see me: "But sometimes I don't think he's really here at all. He's like a wind or a fire, not a person. Like Odysseus."

— *the long trill went on and on, the piano strained high, high, touching the sky* — "Jesus Christ!" he said. "Why do you have to be deaf to write such great music?" And I saw he'd been crying. It wasn't like him. He was always the one with no emotions. The brick-walled one.

"All right, Claudius. Get your clothes on. You and I are going to drive to Hyannis. Right now."

"How come?" But his face lit up. I sat up on the bed and threw open the shutters. Light exploded across the waxed oak floor... "Do we have to wait for the others?"

"No." He was really smiling now, but he looked like he hadn't had any sleep. "Look, Odysseus wanted a souvenir, didn't he? Maybe we can get him something really nice, and then maybe he'll go away."

Downstairs, Laura's record clicked.
***

In the afternoon Sandy made me drive him and Odysseus to Lura's grave, which was five miles past the last of Charley's Cliffs. Claude had already hidden the parcel we had bought in my den, in the desk drawer under the typewriter...

We were in our ancient Austin, with Claude nestled against me as if terrified, and Odysseus in the front seat too, watching the view, and Sandy in the doggie seat. Claude pushed hard against me the whole time. Odysseus seemed preoccupied: his eyes flitted from cliff to pebble strewn roadside to forest wall. We took a left into the cemetery and I saw the grave.

I walked ahead, not wanting to be too close to the stranger, and Claude was huddled against me the whole time. The cement path was broken by moss-veins and tufts of grass, and the sun shone so fiercely that the newer gravestones, the ones that had been washed recently, blazed blindingly.

Claude whispered, "Do you think it'll work? The present, I mean." We walked on quickly so as to be out of earshot.

"For thirty-nine ninety-five," I said, "It better." Then I said, "Christ, I'm scared." We came up to the grave and stopped suddenly. I knelt down and saw that there was a clumsy wreath of wild flowers on the ground. "Did you do this?" I asked Claude.

"No." I turned around and saw Sandy; he looked away. And then Odysseus was behind us, his shadow eclipsing the gravestone. Claude said, under his breath, "You shouldn't have brought him here. This is our place."

In the heat-haze, in the oppressive bright stillness, still the stranger's hair caught fire and flamed. Still his tunic rustled; and still his lips moved differently from the sounds we heard…

"Wives," he said, sighing. "I have a wife, too."

"Then why don't you go back to her?" I said, angry. Already he'd lured Sandy into his power and he'd driven Claude to near hysteria. "What's your game, stranger? All right, so you're not an escapee from a mental home, but what do you want from us?"

"Nothing that you would not give freely..."

Sandy said, "I told him about Mom, Harry. We ran down to the very end of DuPertuis Lane this morning, maybe three miles. He loves your sneakers ... I played him Mom's records." His light blue teeshirt was plastered to him, the hair glistening-damp. "He wanted to pour a libation here, that's all." He looked at me, his eyes seeming to conceal nothing.

I picked up the crude wreath and put it on top of the gravestone. The marble had already worn away some; you couldn't read her name unless you got the exact angle of sunlight.

"I have a wife too," said Odysseus. "She sits at home and' weaves enormous tapestries. And sometimes she rips them up, and begin again, and rips them up, and begins again ..."

"Don't you feel sorry for her?" I said.

"No," he said. Not very convincingly, though. "I like the sea and the changings and the constant strangenesses of new shores. To be at home is to be rooted, like rocks, like trees: I don't, feel *real* in that way. Sometimes I feel more like a wind, something, that slips through people's fingers."

"Oh?"

He went on: "You should all be thankful to my wife Penelope, ' though. If she were to stop weaving, you'd all come to an end, : most likely ... because a millennium or two ago she was sick of all those scenes of heroes and titans and beasts. She became a little: more creative, a little...how do you people say it these days ... science-fictional. And everything she weaves comes true, of I course."

"That's bullshit," I said. "The world has existed far longer than your Greek mythology ever did..."

"When a good writer writes, doesn't the story seem to stretch beyond the writing itself? Don't the characters seem to have histories from long before the first page? But they don't you know."

Claude said, "So did you spring into being when Homer sang, then, Odysseus?" Odysseus' face clouded for a moment. Then he said: "Homer?" He seemed very puzzled. "Now who is that?"

"You can't see where you come from," Claude said, "unless you stand outside where you came from."

Odysseus said in a hurry, "Let's talk of other things. It hurts me to think of my wife alone at her loom. I've never stopped feeling guilty ... you know, one of you boys should come with me when I leave."

He said it so casually. It was much too impromptu. I knew at once that this was why he had come. I stared at my two boys, and saw they were both terrified.

"But think of it!" Odysseus cried out. "Think of the open sea, the wind on the wine-dark waves, the giants and the cyclopes and the golden princesses and the enchantresses...and of being immortal. For we are not real as you are; we are more than that. We are the old things that do not change."

"I won't leave my father," said Claude hesitantly.

"I'll say you won't!" I said.

We all looked at Sandy. He was so small... Suddenly Claude said, "Maybe one of *us* is meant to go. If so, I'll go, Dad. If one of us has to. I know you'll never want to lose Sandy, and it's the only way."

"Hold it, kid!" I said. "No one's going anywhere! Except Odysseus. He's going straight back to the nuthouse. "

Sandy was shaking with anger, struggling to get something out, and then — "Fuck you Odysseus!" he screamed. "Leave us alone! Just get out of our lives, just fuck off!"

In the appalling silence I saw (Laura's arms, anger-hammering the dead piano, Laura tearing the music, Laura's eyes from the coffin depths-) — Sandy backing away into the dead stone.

"It's all right," Odysseus said gently. "I don't insist..."

And then there was more silence. And behind the silence, from behind the cliffs across Moore Avenue, came the whisper of the unseen sea.

***

And so in the evening we went to the beach and sat on the sand and ate broiled hamburgers and watched the sun setting behind us, partly over the cliffs, partly over Tuckatinck Island, a little over the open sea.

He was going to leave in the morning.

After the afternoon's explosions I just wanted to relax. I knew that he was leaving and that there was nothing to worry about anymore ... Odysseus sat with his feet just touching the water, telling tall tales. He looked out to sea the whole time; and though I knew his ship was meant to be docked by the island, I still could see nothing. Only a haze that enveloped the rocks and rose and shifted in color from white to blue-gray, like a Siamese cat's fur.

We were waiting for Claude. Sandy was away in the water, jumping up and down.

Claude came clutching the parcel. running out of the house. He made a breeze with his running, he made the sand fly, for a moment I thought he was Sandy.

"So you still don't see my ship?" Odysseus was saying. "Your son there, he does."

Claude crashed down beside us. The sand poured into my cutoffs...he thrust the parcel at me. I caught his eye for a moment. His look said, This won't work.

"Come back, Sandy!" I hollered. "We've got something to do!" He ran over the dark waves, a dark streak in the pink and gray...and tumbled in front of us. Sand and water on my face.

"We're sorry to see you go." It was a ritual. The words were meaningless.

"I know you are not," said Odysseus, not playing the game.

I handed him the parcel wordlessly.

He opened it and took out the sneakers...soft suede Adidases" fawn with pale blue stripes, size ten, nesting on layers of tissue...he seemed very thoughtful.

"Thank you," he said. There was so much sadness in his voice. "I will wear them often, when I tread strange shores, and I will think of your beautiful children, the ones who would not come with me, the ones who loved their father better than the wild wide ocean."

"Tell us another story," said Sandy. "Tell us about Troy."

"You don't want to hear about it." A wind had sprung up; for once the billowing of his hair seemed to match reality. He stroked the sneakers. Behind the habitual coldness of his eyes I thought I saw ... some indescribable yearning. It was truly terrible, and I was afraid.

"I can show you," he said, "the fires of Troy, I can show you if you can see them. Look there at the island, over by the ship..." And all I could see was the shifting haze, more pink now in the twilight.

"Don't you see the fire across the wine-dark sea?" said Odysseus. "Don't you see the slaughter, don't you see the screaming women being dragged to the ships?"

The haze twisted. But I saw nothing.

Then Sandy burst out: "I see it all, Harry! I see everything! I see the walls crumbling and the horse standing behind the walls, and the fire burning the houses and the children screaming in the streets...."

"Cut the crap, Sandy!" said Claude tightly. He was trembling all over. "Your son has vision, then," Odysseus said. "He is like one of us ..."

Sandy said, "It's terrible, Harry! Now they've dragged a child from its mother, they're going to throw it down from the walls, and the walls are falling, falling—"

The sky was fire blood-red, but I saw nothing — Claude was shaking Sandy. "It's all lies, Dad! He's just making it up! He doesn't see those things!" he screamed. And Sandy's eyes were frozen like Laura's eyes, crystallized and cold, watching me from the coffin —

I put out my arms and covered the boy's eyes. He pushed me way. "I've got to see, Harry, I've got to!" he whispered. And I saw that Odysseus no longer seemed interested in us. He had stood up and had put on his new sneakers and was springing lightly up and down on them, laughing for joy.

Red rays like fire fingers grasping the water

"This is enough," I said. I lifted Sandy up in my arms. He held me so tightly I couldn't breathe.

"Harry," he said, "you've got to come running with me."

I saw that Claude had gone into the house, and so I walked Sandy to the front of the house, where our

sneakers were, and then we set off down Delenda
Circle, into the red-streaked darkness.

It was hard at first. Mostly I watched the
pavement. When I looked up Sandy was running
free, pounding the ground and leaping in smooth
curves and looking straight ahead. The woods were
so much taller than him. We crossed Moore Avenue
and turned into DuPertuis Lane.

"Don't tailgate!" Sandy hollered.

We ran on. I felt lost in the leaf-moist stillness. The
rhythm of foot-thuds became a heartbeat. We ran flat
out and the lane corkscrewed, it was alive, it was a
snake's gullet, we were flowing into its gut, flowing
like blood, like bile.

"Wait for me, damn it!" I shouted.

He was into the wood now, darting from shadow
to shadow, and I was so tired I could hardly think.
My sneakers crunched on twigs and winced away
from pebbles.

And then we stopped.

Why had he made me do this? Later I realized: he
was showing me that he possessed me. That I
belonged to him, no matter what.

We sank down on the wet ground, against a tree.

Sandy said, "Dad."

He said it shyly. He wasn't used to calling me
Dad. But defiantly too. Because I *was* his father. He
shook something out of his hair and smoothed a
crease in his teeshirt and a moonbeam fell on his
face…

Even in this darkness his eyes could still flash, like sunlight out of a gap in a thundercloud. I waited. It was his show. I didn't know what was coming. It could have been a storm. Or nothing at all.

— Laura's eyes breaking out from behind the crook of the piano —

"Dad, will you love me forever?"

"Of course, Sandy," I said, tense.

"And Claude? You're going to stop pushing him away froIn you?"

"I don't know what you mean," I lied.

A leaf fell.

"Christ, Dad…can't you think of her as a human being? Can't you remember the human things about her? I make you think of her, don't I, Dad? But she isn't real anymore. And I don't think I am, either… you never did see the ship, did you, Dad, or the fire from the sea…?" .

"Let's talk about something else," I said.

The forest pressed us in. We really were in the serpent's gut. And Sandy seemed so far away. Even though I could smell the fabric softener on his tee-shirt, through the sweet odor of boy sweat.

"I have to go with Odysseus, Dad."

"No, Sandy, please," I said, "don't play games with me, you'll kill me …"

"I saw the ship. I saw the walls crumble. I saw the fire." He spoke without emotion. "I'm part of his world, Harry, But that's not why I have to go."

I waited.

"If I stay here I'm going to go on breaking your heart, forever," he said, talking into the ground.

"How can you say that?" I said.

"You're so ashamed about feeling one way about me and one way about Claude. Your guilt's a scary thing. And it's only that you're afraid of him... because he's so like you. People think they love the things they can't be. That's all you see in me, Dad."

He had drained me. I couldn't talk. All I could think of was him, leaping from diving rocks, running in the darkness, sliding down the banisters ...

"Daddy, before I go, I have a gift for you too."

This was his gift: he laughed me Laura's laugh until the trees laughed in the close darkness, until his laughing dried up, and then I caught the laugh from him and laughed too, laughed hysterically until I couldn't stop crying.

Then he said, "Let's go, Dad."

In the moonlight I saw that his lips didn't match his words.

***

There's a little bit of the stereotype that's true. I do possess a tattered notebook and I do go around writing in it: lines that become poems, sometimes, but usually are just lines that go nowhere, smoke-trails of a skywriter that disperse in the wind...

I carried the notebook out to the beach.

I saw two sets of sneaker prints. Size ten and size six.

They led to a point in the sand and stopped.

"I think the stranger was Death," I whispered to myself.

Claude said, startling me — I didn't know he was there —"No, Daddy, no. Sandy went away because he loved us. To kill your mourning, to give me a chance." He looked so serious. He hadn't slept.

As we looked out at the sea a high wind sprang up and blew the fog away from Tuckatinck Island, and the fog drifted, skimming the water still, toward the sunrise, blushing against the gray sea and sky.

"It's the ship!" Claude yelled. And he jumped up and down frantically and waved, "Goodbye, goodbye, Sandy!" and rushed out into the low tide…

"Do you see the ship?" I called out to him.

"No."

We turned and went into the house. Claude had left the record on. The one of Laura playing the opus one one one.

Jesus Christ! Do you have to be deaf to write great music?

And then I saw that we are all deaf, and blind too. If we were not, if we could see, we would be like Sandy. We wouldn't need visions, or art. We would run after the truth until we melted into a breeze, into sea water, into sunlight.

That's why art is all lies.

I saw my son in the doorway, I thought he was Sandy for a moment. Then I crushed him against me as though it were the last time.

Claude said, "I'm not Sandy, Dad, but some day..." behind the grief, his eyes sparkled briefly ... "someday, can we go running in the woods?"

I wrote another line in the book:

art is the dark glasses a blind man wears

— *Cape Cod and Arlington, 1978*

THE BAD NEWS EXPRESS

This story originally appeared under a different title, but I think this one is snappier and more expressive. Completists should note that this version contains a number of revisions.

What if Ingmar Bergman had directed The Bad News Bears *— and the whole story took place on the Orient Express? This story offers one possible answer to the above conundrum.*

I saw Euripides' play Alcestis *for the first (and only) time in a school production when I was a student at Eton, in my teens. The play was performed in Greek, and the boy actors all spoke in a muffled sort of way, through masks; nevertheless, the tragicomic drama made an impression on me. Although, I must confess, I didn't understand a word of it; I studied Greek later, on my own, and still read it only with difficulty.*

Death is a character in Alcestis *as it is in this short story. When the theme of fathers and sons is raised, one can't help thinking of death, because one's children are, in a very real sense, a kind of last-ditch effort to avoid the extinction of the self. Death is an off-stage presence in the other three stories too. I don't like death. It really scares me. Maybe I should hurry up and have a son.*

we know that death is evil
if death were good
the gods themselves would die   — Sappho

what? death has a sense of humor? —Euripides,
                              Alcestis

The Bad News Express

When I think back to the year when I was twelve and we all skipped school and rode the rails all over Europe with the parents muttering on about value-readjustments and expanding our experiential cosmos-

I see Dad, farting to death on the Athens-Paris Express. And the crammed air getting stinkier and stinkier, and the fields of Yugoslavia unreeling like a sickly-green cloth-roll, and I hear Mom's knit-knit-knitting. And Sophie too, knit-knit-knitting like a wee color Xerox, them with their black hair bunned up and their dresses faded green floral prints and Sophie with those pink shreds of leftover yarn juryrigging her pigtails...

I'm a hell of a lot older now, and I've read books that tell you how the light falls on the ruins at Sounion and stuff like that. Yah. Jesus. I saw it. It wasn't like that at all. It was — think of the sky as a bright blue safe dropping from a cosmic skyscraper. That's the thing I remember. The ruins ... take 'em or leave 'em. But the sky and then the mists at Delphi in the dawn. Creepy. Oh, Greece, Greece, Greece. I'm going to go back.

After Greece the world got sick. I mean, Dad got
sicker and sicker and I knew that dying wasn't
anything like in *Love Story*. It's as glamorous as a
garbage can in the Bronx.

It's nervousness. It's wondering how tactless you
can get. It's sitting in nonsmoking compartments in
cramped European trains and not daring to get up
and leave because he'll think you don't love him. It's
the fart that makes you cry.

And it was so inconvenient. Because that year I
was posed to be at home and practicing to be a hitter
for whatever team I wanted to be a hitter for at the
time even though I couldn't hit worth shit. And my
world was falling in ruins all around me as we
traipsed like demons from hotel to demi-pension to
inn to YMCA to sleeping cars.

It was so hard to believe he was dying. Dad looked
like a seedy stevedore from Naples — which is just
what *his* Dad was, but in real life he was Professor
Emilio Caro and taught comparative lit at some
college round the corner and had a string of PhD's
that stretched all the way from Cambridge,
Massachusetts, to Cambridge, England. Yah. In the
compartment he'd have the whole of the seat that
was facing the way the train was going all to himself
so he could stretch out. And he'd erupt now and
then like a noisy volcano spewing brimstone. When
he was better he'd sit back and pontificate. It was
like that all the way through Yugoslavia.

Mom was Greek and just beautiful. I look a lot like
her, but I'm just wiry and muscly enough to look

cute and not too faggy. If she didn't wear those shabby clothes, and if she didn't sit there just knitting, her eyes downcast, not even noticing her four-year-old daughter's awkward mimicking ... I always changed my clothes every few hours. I was compulsive about it. And frankly, I was scared because of all the fart gas, thinking it might have germs.

It's so hard to be afraid of being near your own father. The train wasn't like Amtrak. No way. There were these corridors down the side and individualized compartments with seats like the sofas you donate to the Salvation Army.

When I could-like pretending to go to the bathroom — I'd stalk the corridors. I'd lean out of the windows until I almost fell out or until the guard caught me or until the krauts from the next compartment came out to jabber and smoke. They always treated me like I wasn't there. Well, I was a kid. I was used to shoving off.

A couple hours from the Austrian border and we'd just trundled past one of those Hollywood villages, a little grimier than the brochure, and I was leaning out again and thinking about Greece and baseball and death —

Like, you know, Greece and death. There was this play we saw at Epidauros, there was this drama festival there...it was called Alcestis and it was by Euripides. There was this guy Admetos, see, who'd gotten Death to agree to let him off if he could find someone else to buy it in his place. So he got his own wife. Then his friend Heracles (that's Hercules to you philistines) came visiting just in time for the funeral, and he got so mad that he went down to the underworld and wrestled Death to the ground (just like those FBI agents. Yah.) So they all got off scot free. That was a weird idea and it gave me a nightmare at the hotel. With Dad dying and all. They wore these masks and their voices came echo-howling round and round the enormous arena and the mask for Death was worse than something out of *The Exorcist* ....

And baseball? Well. There was this kid called Chet Perkins the Pumpkin who pitched for the Annandale Coca-Cola Tomcats or something. He was (as Dad said in a more lucid moment) "querulous, belligerent, beady-eyed and hirsute." (I wrote it down. Dad's pontifications were pretty damn funny sometimes, when you forgot he was on the verge of croaking.) When he got on the field he turned into a blubbery Baryshnikov, though, and so when he beaned me I knew it was no accident. Next season I was going to bust the Pumpkin into a gooey pulp. So what if they sent me off the field.

Well — I had my head in the wind and my hair was all tangled and dusty and billowing and I was pressed hard against the train and the chugchugging and it felt, you know, sexy ... I felt a stab in the ribs and nearly fell out.

"Don't do that, dummy!" I gasped.

"Mommy wants you back, Jody."

"Sophie—"

"Yeah, I know. I'm a pain in the ath," she chirped sweetly. I slid the door panel open and watched the point of light whisk across the peeling varnish...

"I'm here, Mom." They'd been fighting.

I could tell by the tongue-bitten pent-up smile that froze on Mom's face. I could tell by Dad's staring fixedly out of the window as if the telegraph poles were lines of Dante or pictures of naked women. And the smell hit me hard.

"Yah, can I get Dad something?" I said. "No. I just thought it'd be nice if we were all together, Jody," Mom said, and went on with her knitting.

In a few minutes Dad had fallen asleep, and the snoring and the farting began to syncopate with the chugging of the train, like progressive jazz. Sophie suddenly conked out too. This travelling was a bit much for a kid like that sometimes. And the sun was setting ahead of us somewheres, making the meadows all eerie and bloody.

So it was just me and Mom awake then and I knew something was going to happen. I knew she was going to tell me something. We had a special thing going, me and Mom. Going to Greece had confirmed it somehow. Because ... I had recognized everything there. I mean like the incredible blueness of the sky. I mean knew it was the way things are meant to be, and that the smog over Brooklyn and even the sun shining through the palms of Florida ... were just imitations. We'd lived in so many places and none of them had ever been home. And this was. Sophie and Dad — well, they were the wop contingent. I'm allowed to say that because I am one, too. "What were you fighting about?" Mom said, "Do you remember Alcestis?"

"The play in Epidauros?"

"Uh huh." Knit-knit. And the sunset in her eyes. "What would you say if I took Dad's place?" , I started. "He'd never let you!" I said. She shushed me quickly and pointed to Dad, who was snoring and smiling in his sleep. "Well he wouldn't, would he?" I whispered. "Anyway you're just torturing yourself over it. Life isn't a play by Euripides, Mom."

"I guess."

"The man in the play was an asshole."

"I guess." Knit. We didn't talk for an hour after that. I was really disturbed because she'd talked almost like it were possible to switch around and die instead of someone else. I tried to forget about it and sat there in the smelly dark, imagining myself batting the Pumpkin's pitches into his face and the blood spurting. Jesus. Yah. So we got to the Austrian border and the train stopped for us to get our papers stamped, and then I had to help Dad go to the bathroom. Well — this old man and this kid come charging out from a cubicle in the station and you know what they're thinking, those slimy *Passkontrollebeamterscheissekopf* characters with their glittertacky uniforms and pug faces. Yah, dying isn't glamorous at all. I thought that all the way back to the compartment. It's dirty and disgusting and gross.

***

Later — we were stalled at the station for a couple of hours — me and Dad were talking on a bench together. He was wrapped in a gray fur coat even though it was the middle of night. He had his arm around me and I was uneasy. I remember the bench: one of the planks was missing from the seat and it had a green lacquery look in the harsh station lights ...

"Dad," I said, "Mom just made a really weird suggestion." (1 remembered the Greek chorus moving like dancing dolls across the proscenium... and Death's face. In the nightmare the face would jump up at me and stare me down. There were times when I saw the mask of Death almost emerging from behind Dad's face...)

"Your momma very weird, *ragazzo*," Dad said in his best spaghetti-sauce-commercial accent that always made me laugh, only I didn't; and then I was afraid his feelings would be hurt so I forced out a chuckle that choked me.

"But what exactly did she mean?" I said, persisting.

"Your mother's a witch, you know. Your grandad always tried to ward off the evil eye when she came to their house. At first. I thought she was going to stop all that —"

He looked at me and then stopped talking, as though he'd said too much. "What am I saying, *ragazzo?*" he said. "I shouldn't be sitting here badmouthing my own wife now, should I? Well I take it back. She's no witch ... even though she thinks she is … but she's headstrong, strong-willed, wilful, foolhardy."

"That was a clever thing to say, Dad," I said, filing it away.

"Verbal concatenations are cool, aren't they?" he said, taking a slug from one of those funny teeny continental Coke bottles.

"Especially beginning each word with the previous final syllable …"

I hugged him. It was hard. It seemed like under the big coat there was nothing at all, an emptiness. It felt almost as though he were dissolving under the pressure of my arms. He handed rne the bottle and I had to have some, even though it made me queasy.

A breeze whooshed over and lifted the stench a little. "So what did you think about Momma's proposal?" he said.

"Dad, you'd never let her anyway! I know you, Daddy! Admetos was an asshole."

Was it the glare from the overhead sodium arcs?

He wouldn't meet my eyes and I didn't want him to try.

***

The train rumbled into the dark night. It was our second night on the Express; Sophie and I shared one cabin of the sleeping car and Mom and Dad had one about four cabins down. We sat in Second Class in the daytime, understand…but with Dad sick we couldn't compromise about the sleeper.

Well, I couldn't sleep. The moon shone into the cabin which wasn't more than a cubbyhole, and I couldn't close the blinds because it was kind of a night light for Sophie. So I got down from the top bunk and changed my clothes a couple of times and washed my face and hands in the midget basin that only ran cold water, like I wanted to scrub every last germ into oblivion. I'd look into the mirror over the basin and comb my hair over and over. Finally I got out my baseball bat from the satchel and swung a couple of times, and then stuffed it back into the bag.

You'll never be any good, I told me, *in spite of the fancy aluminum bat and the spiffy satchel and the classy fifty dollar mitt that two months on an uphill paper route earned you.*

I went outside in a holey tee-shirt and pyjama bottoms.

Mom was there. She was leaning out of the window the way I always did. That pleased me no end, that we had so much in common, even our secret pleasures.

I stood watching her for a while. She didn't know I was there and she was sort of moaning and talking to herself. It was in Greek and I don't know Greek except bad words like *skatá*. For some reason the mask of Death came floating to the top of my mind. I choked it back but I must have cried out, because she saw me then. She said something to me, so softly I had to strain to hear anything above the patter of the train. I crept up closer to her.

She smelled sweet-and-sour, like old oranges.

There was a full moon and it turned up the contrast on her, so her hair was like liquid coal and her face like chalk and her eyes like onyxes polished into cabochons. I could see her figure through the nightgown and I remember it was really firm and strong-looking, not like a forty-year-old woman's at all.

"It's time for me to tell you the family secret, Jody sweetheart," she said, so faintly that it was almost an overtone of the wind that the train made, "and about myths and truths."

"Sure, shoot," I said. I thought she just needed a quiet listener who wouldn't bug her; and I was good at that. Her husband was dying and I knew how it was.

Also, I was scared stiff and I was ready to listen to any kind of voice at all.

"Do you know why we went to Greece?"

"Sure," I said. "To see grandma and grandpa and the other Vlachapouloses and...well..." Jesus. I thought of the sky falling from the sky and the blue that was bluer than blue and I knew that was the real reason for me but I wouldn't ever be able to talk about it, not even with her.

"There was another reason," she said. "Okay. A lot of people think myths are just stories. They are, mostly—but they all come from somewhere. Did you know that my family claims descent from the royal house of Admetos?"

Suddenly I could hear my own heart pounding above the train-roar, suddenly I knew I was shaking all over and —

She was saying, "It's not like in Euripides. That's just a distorted memory of the truth. There were things called Mysteries that only initiates knew about in those days, mostly mumbojumbo about symbolic death and rebirth: well, I'm a Priestess of the Mysteries."

"Dad said you were a witch!" I blurted out.

She laughed very lightly and I couldn't tell if it wasn't the rattle of a chain in the train or the clang of a distant shutter ..."

"Sure, baby. Italians are very superstitious."

She touched my cheek and her hand was ice cold. Or maybe I was burning with fear.

I heard her say, "Our family...and that includes you, and that's why you have to know this, because I'm going to go away, soon —" *I'm not hearing this* I thought *I'm not. I'm not.* "—— Our family has the blood of Admetos in its veins, we all have the power to cheat Death, to trade places with other people... because we understand Death. You can see Death whenever you want to, Jody, whenever you look into a mirror and stare, past your own face, into the face within ... well, I've decided to do it."

"Dad'll never let you!" I said fiercely. "Admetos was an asshole! Nobody would let the person they love commit suicide —" And I didn't believe it. I *couldn't* believe it.

And underneath I knew it was as true as the blue of the sky over the Cape of Sounion, as true as the mask of Death, as true as the morning mist that tendriled the broken columns at Delphi....

Yah. I'd stared at mirrors before.

I knew I carried Death inside me and I could will myself to face it. I knew that there were secret words that lay in my unconscious, spells that I could use. If the moment came.

I could hear her talking through the tumble of my heartbeat. She was saying how they'd made a mutual decision and how it was better for the kids otherwise she couldn't afford to send them to college on her earnings as a secretary-

She went on talking but it was the chattering of the train like teeth death rattle of wheels iron on iron chittering of unoiled chains thunder of the wind scream dinning in my head —

I made it to the cabin. I slid the door with a slam. I listened to myself breathing. Slower. Slower. Remote.

How could you do it, Dad? I wanted to bawl like a baby and nothing came. I glanced up and the mirror glared back, taunting. I turned to face the wall and it was metal and I saw my eyes reflected like ghost eyes, eyes of Death and I squeezed them shut, to shut out the eyes, and plastered the blanket over my face and I, I —

Suffocating in the dark for the whole night, I couldn't sleep because I knew I'd dream and the mask would come for me —

***

Morning broke all at once. We were pushing through mountains and the train kept jerking to a halt and hauling slowly, off-rhythm...I found I'd been hugging my baseball glove like a teddy hear.

I took Sophie over to the dining car. We passed the parents' cabin and I walked very quickly. They'd opened the windows and the air smelled of drifting leaves and cold showers. We found a table with a white starchy tablecloth and a plastic vase with a pink rose, half-wilted.

I was facing the wrong way and I was uneasy. But I tried to pretend like there was nothing wrong. For Sophie's sake.

"*Zwei Apfelsaft*," I said to the waiter. "*Spiegeleier. Speck.*" I pointed to the places on the menu, worn as an old papyrus under the slimy plastic cover, because I knew I'd pronounced it all wrong.

The waiter mumbled something I didn't catch. *Ah well*, I thought, *he has an Austrian accent*. The train was running more smoothly now; a soft pink dawn played over us across the rose-tinted peaks...

I saw Dad in the doorway. A smell of stale apples ... He stood there without moving. The coat was gone. He was wearing fresh clothes. Something was wrong.

"Dad—"

"Jesus, Mary and Joseph," he said — not in the funny accent —" she's done it, I can't think —" He started crying. I'd never heard that before. It didn't sound real. It sounded like the squeaking of the train wheels —

I got up. I was angry. I was hot all over. I stomped over to him. He looked healthy as hell and I thought his crying was phoney and I wished he were dead. He was an asshole just like in the play. I stared up at him and I knew I was scaring him.

"I don't know how you managed to do it," I said. Quietly. "I used to think you were God sometimes, you with your clever colorful phrases and all. But you made her die. Maybe you can live with it. Fuck you."

He'd stopped crying now and his eyes looked like stone. He just gaped at me. *"Ragazzo,"* he said, "God damn it, we need each other now. We made a logical decision, it was all for you kids, we weren't thinking about anything else. Christ, do you think I feel supercool about this or something?"

"Why should I comfort you? I'm your kid, not your mother!" I yelled. Then I pushed past him and went running to their cabin and pulled the door open.

Their cabin was a mirror image of mine; they made them back to back to save on rivets. The walls were metal like ours. The bunks —

I saw her on the lower bunk. She wasn't dead yet. Shit — was still breathing. But something had gone from her. Even though it was broad daylight now the contrast was still turned up on her, as though a different light, a moon-drenched pale light, shone over her…

The white face hid a hint of sky blue.

"Mom," I whispered.

I bent over to kiss the closed eyes. I felt them tremble a little. Then I turned around and saw the mirror over the basin —

You know how in the old days they stuck a mirror over your face to see if your were still alive? They're always doing that in Sherlock Holmes movies…

— breath stains frosting the glass so I could only just see my own face blurring and melting —

(Behind the frost, the train purred past mountains softly furred with green. The brightness hurt. I went and drew the shutters.)

I stared into the mirror. I stared at it angry, because I'd never been angrier in my life. Dad had done the wrong thing. You don't let people die in your place. I wasn't thinking about our family's future and how hard they must have fought over it. I just knew it was wrong.

— the frosting shifted, unfocused, shifted —

My own irises through the mist. Alien. Cold.

I knew she was going fast. In a few hours the spell would be one way. And I was starting to know other things too. I was starting to remember things. Words were welling up behind the dam of my unconscious.

Things I had known all the time.

I hurled all the anger I could dredge up at those eyes. I was going to pull her out of there. My eyes stared back, concentrating my anger.

"Come and get me'" I screamed and the thing inside me leapt clear of me and fell swirling down the irises that spun and twisted and there were tunnels and tunnels and they were skull eyes walled by patches of white bone graying into terrible blackness —

Cold. Cold.

Faintly the train rumbled still.

I guess each person has his own private death. All the images and things he's most afraid of, everything he's pushed down to the very bottom of his mind —

Cold and darkness.

Then cold and light; moonlight without a moon, and I saw I was in a spotlight walking on a field of springy skulls, as though each one were attached to a bedspring, bobbing up and down as I trod. It was an eerie bouncy smoothness…

Then a voice that came from all around me. In a language I didn't know. But I understood it perfectly:

Who *art* thou, that darest enter?

The voice was echo-shifted so I couldn't tell where it came from, it sprang out of the darkness and it made a cold wind with a whiff of methane and rotten egg gas. I suddenly knew the answer to that question, and I spoke a stream of gibberish that sounded like this *gispesimikyeuranuasterondos* and I knew it was Greek:

I am a child of earth and of starry heaven.

It came out in a blurry kind of way and I was trying to stop myself from howling or screaming or wetting myself, it was that bad. It was a tall deep darkness and I knew it stretched to forever. The voice asked me more questions and I answered in the same gibberish and sometimes I knew what it meant but sometimes I didn't and it went on for it seemed like hours —

Then *bam!* A flight of stairs in the spotlight and banisters with bony fingers quivering and cohwebs and I walked up it. My own steps. Ping. Ping. Metallic, distant. And the heartbeat. And so far away it was almost like sea waves lapping — the kettledrum of train on mountainside …

I was scared. Shitless. But I was so angry. There was something fake about all this. It was too plastic, too like a horror movie. I knew I had to walk up the steps and I did, and the light patch grew a little and there was the music of harps, dry and dissipating quickly into the dusty darkness.

"So you like my show?" A low voice inside my head. I saw him. The skull face. And purple tights and a green cape and the Greek letter theta in a circle on his chest.

He was standing on a landing on a kind of mezzanine and the harp players were at his feet and they were skeletons and harps of bone with prows of ghoul faces and red crystal eyes. And a low wind moaning. And a chorus sighing. And a string orchestra, sort of a sneering, trilling ostinato of high-pitched squeaks …

"I asked you a question, kid."

"I think it's…" What did you say to Death? "I think it's phoney, damn it! Give me my mother back!"

There. I'd said it. Now he'd take me and I'd live down here forever.

"Well, well, well," said Death. A grin widened and faded out. "I've seen a lot of people like you…selfish people, the lot of you. Always wanting something. Preferably for nothing."

"I can pay!" I said. "You can come and get me instead! I'm from the blood of Admetos and the bargain stands still, the bargain you made with him —"

"Don't give me that shit," said Death. "I'll do whatever I please." But he was shaking. Maybe there *was* a chink in his armor.

I looked him over. I was scared, sure, but somehow not as badly as I thought I'd be. I was more scared when I didn't know what to expect … the music and the skulls were spooky hut plastic. "So bring her back to life."

"Cod, you're insufferable!" he said, then he did a hideous cackle. I'd been expecting one for a while, so I stood firm and didn't let it faze me. "If I let her go now, I'm still going to have to collect sometime, you know that. Besides, I don't bargain. It's a fixed price store here."

"Heracles didn't think that when he wrestled you to the ground."

"I'd like to see you try."

I stood and listened to the wind. The wind howled but I didn't feel anything. It was dry and cold. When I spoke the air frost ed. As I watched him he shimmered and changed into the actor at Epidauros with the mask of Death. It was like the nightmare, close up. The skull face was dead white and the eyes were dead and I couldn't read them…

"Okay," said Death. "If you're going to stand there forever. I suppose we might work out a little something. I don't get much amusement here. I don't suppose you wrestle, but — how about something else?"

"I thought I was just supposed to stay here and you would go wake her up," I said slowly. The cackle came again. I wasn't afraid anymore. I was in this and I was going to fight it out till the end.

"I love children," he said. "They're so illogical. You won't he around to enjoy her if you die, will you? What would be the point? Oh, don't give me that bull about love and compassion. I don't understand things like that. They don't pay me for my empathy quotient. Anyhow, if you stay here, when your sister grows up she'll come looking for you. She's got the power too, you know. And she adores you."

"How do you know?" Suddenly I felt proud of Sophie. As I'd never done before. I thought of her without me and —

"Play chess?" he said suddenly.

"You saw *The* Seventh Seal?" Mom and Dad always made me watch the serious movies on channel 26. (Expand your *experiential* cosmos-)

"Shit yes. I always watch every movie where I'm the big hero."

"The way I interpreted it you were more like the bad guy. Anyways, I don't play chess."

"...Monopoly?"

"Uh uh."

"Too bad." He started to shimmer again, as though to change shape, then changed his mind and stayed as the play actor..."I've got it! This dude called Orpheus came by once, and...you sing?"

"Oh sure, I tried out for the Brooklyn Boys Chorus and I shattered a 69¢ Burger King glass."

"Oh, get out of here," said Death.

"Baseball?" I said faintly...and tried to choke it back but I knew I'd said it and I was in for it now and as if to play up my helplessness, the music of strings and harp welled up and the moan of the wind shrilled to a shriek —

"That's it!" said Death briskly. He clapped his hands.

Suddenly I saw that we were overlooking a field of plastic looking grass and that there were tiers and tiers of spectators and the train rumbling suddenly turned into the murmur of a crowd —

"I'll put your mother on third base," he said. I saw her there.

She stood still like a statue and even at the distance I could see how beautiful she was and how the light on her was still moonlight even under the gathering sunlight that was breaking overhead and the sun was yellow and had eyes and a frown like in a kid's painting. "I'll put your Dad on first; he's got farther to go because after all he started it all. Now all you have to do is..."

He took off his mask.

It was Chet Perkins, the Pumpkin. Handing me the expensive bat I'd carried with me across Europe and hadn't used once.

I looked at his slits of eyes squinting at me and his body shaking like a jello that's been left out too long and I hated him. He shimmered back into his superhero costume but now it was topped by a green and purple baseball cap with the big theta on it. Theta for thanatos. The skull face scrutinized me. I saw right through the eyes into the old landing with the ghouls playing harps and I knew that our pavilion overlooking the baseball field was a fakery on top of a fakery.

Then I turned around and looked at the field and the crowd screaming began to make me feel funny and warm inside and I knew I wanted to do whatever it was, even if I died trying ….

I felt Death's breath in my back. Cold and slimy.

"Okay, *ragazzo*," he said, and he suddenly sounded like my Dad and made me twist my intestines…"All you have to do is hit a home run. And I'm pitching."

I gripped the bat and started walking down the steps, J could see that it was like five hundred steps down to the grass meadow and the sun was hurting my eyes —

Death called after me: "How about second base? Did you have anyone in mind?"

"No," I said, not looking back. I didn't even want to think about it. Aunt Rosie? Poor old Granddad who died of a surfeit of booze? I tried to push the thought back as far as I could. I took three more steps and I heard Death taunting me.

"You humans are all alike!" he cackled. "Selfish, selfish, selfish. Just think what's in your power! You could bring back anyone to life — Jesus Christ, Einstein, Shakespeare —

I turned around. "Damn it, I don't give a shit about I hose people! I'm just a kid who wants his family to stay in one piece!"

"Charity begins at home, eh?"

"Fuck you!"

***

I sort of came to. I saw the tiers all around stretching as far as I could see but sometimes there were holes in the tiers and I saw blackness through them lanced by eerie light. They were like living backcloth, in a seedy off-off-Broadway theater or something, that hadn't been used in a long long time.

I was holding the bat, my own bat, and it was a little-league sized field so I saw Death in his super-costume standing pretty near and licking his chops.

"Where's the catcher?" I yelled.

Death vanished. I swirled round. He stood behind me and I got a whiff of his foul breath as he burst into a villainous campy laugh. "You could do with a good mouthwash," I said. Then I hefted the bat and waited. The crowd's murmur was the same as the pounding of the train...the tiers of living people so I knew it was all a backcloth now. And a wind gusted through the gaps, icy and fetid as Death himself.

I wanted to go find the locker room and scrub myself into *pieces* before I came on. But I was there and the crowd was screaming and I saw Mom and Dad, but I saw right through them so I knew they were shades of people, and the sun shone fierce as anything making me blink over and over and it was cold as shit ... "

Chet Perkins was up there doing his fancy warm up and —

Zing! Talk about a fast ball. I was still waiting for it when I heard the s-s-t-r-r-r-i-ke *ONE!*

I knew it was all a set up now. I knew it was going to be a dirty game all the way. Death vanished and popped up all over the field, here an outfielder there a shortstop, and then he'd guffaw and snicker and giggle and the crowd up there would copy him. I looked closer and saw they were all —

Ghosts. Zombies. Headless torsos. Withered shrouds with gargoyle faces. Eye sockets dripping rheum. *It's hopeless,* I thought. "God damn it, you've got all the cards," I yelled at Death, who was still in the form of the Pumpkin. "You can make the ball travel faster than light or something and you can rig up this whole Halloween charade to gross me out and give me the creeps..."

"Oh, it's a slow ball you want, huh?" He pitched. I waited. Slow motion. Crowd shrieks dropping an octave like a 78 burbling to a 45 now to 33 now a heart-thump below the threshold of hearing —

The ball hung there for a moment and I saw it was moving dancing in the sunlight, it did three quick

figure-eights and somersaulted into swooping
sweeping curves and zig-zagged like a
hummingbird, hypnotizing me, and then it dangled
in front of me—I swung and it dodged and 1swung
and it dodged me and then it whooshed right past
me into the strike zone and I was still swinging at
nothing —

Thwack! Second strike. Okay. I'd had it. I didn't
want to play anymore.

"Okay, Death," I said. Laughter pealed like funeral
bells. "Ha! You can't take it, can you! Well," Death
said, stalking towards me, "I let this go on because I
wanted to teach you a lesson. You can't win! I am the
great leveler, the ultimate nothing in everyone's life!
I am totally fair! You can't cheat me!" He was
towering over me and his cape was flapping and I
saw the scythe sprout out of his bony hand. "I
represent justice! Justice!" he shouted. "Everyone
dies! Everyone! Everyone!" Holes of eyes burning
blackness —

I dropped my bat and stomped towards him in a
rage. "If you're so fair how come you don't die
yourself, huh?" I screamed. "You're just a God damn
hypocrite! Yah! Jesus!"

He stopped cold. He turned his back on me and
walked over and pluckPd a baseball out of the air.
"Have it your way," he said. He pitched this pathetic
pitch that a first-grader could have handled with a
plastic bat.…

I felt the thunk as I lashed out and then I sprinted
without thinking at all and Death just stood there

without stopping me. I saw the ball fly through a hole in the big canvas crowd and I ran and ran and my Mom reached home plate and vanished and my Dad was puffing like crazy with his fur coat flying and he reached it too I didn't stop I ran I ran I looked up.

On the staircase in the darkness with the harps and wailing strings and the skeletons strumming...Death in his superhero costume on his throne. I stood panting for a while.

Then, "Why'd you let me win?"

Rumble. Rumble. The train. "I don't have to justify myself!" Death grated. Then he looked down and I tried to stare him down but he wouldn't even look at me.

God, I needed a shower!

I said, slowly, "All this crap about justice and the grim reaper and all...all these ghostly sighings and gibbering skeletons and stuff like that...it's not real, is it? You're quite a softie, after all."

He didn't answer. I knew he'd never admit it.

Then I said, "I know why you're so bitter. I can see it so clearly. You want to die so badly but you can't! You have to sit here forever, collecting due debts, like an IRS man or a mafia beater-upper...you're jealous, aren't you?"

He still didn't say anything.

So I walked up to him and touched him lightly on the face. Although it was a skull it felt dry, like skin. And cold. But there was no quiver of breathing. Nothing.

"Gosh," I said, "I wish I could help."

Everyone has his own personal Death locked up inside him. knew this Death; he was part of me and he belonged to me. But I had thrown him into the deepest dungeon of my soul. Of course he was bitter. "I guess I'll have to try to love you, even when it hurts," I said. "After all, I love my Dad even when he farts up such a stink I can't breathe."

"Get out of here already," he said to me.

And so I fell up the irises and into the swirling light and I stepped into the mirror and —

***

There were Mom and Dad sitting on the bunk. Picture perfect. Sophie on Dad's lap. Daylight. A family album portrait.

And Dad said, "Wow, son."

Sheepishly I smiled at the three of them.

"It's gonna be Paris in an hour and we're staying in a hotel on the Champs Elysées," Sophie babbled, "and guess what there's a McDonalds on the Champs Elysées right near the FDR subway cause that's what Daddy says and —"

My mother whispered: *"O child of earth and starry heaven!"* I knew these were words from the ancient ritual of rebirth, from the sacred Mysteries of Eleusis.

And that was it. Because I was too drained to say any more, and they were too emotional to say anything sensible. We were about to start blabbing all at once or be hugging each other in pieces and I couldn't stand a scene like that, not now, no.

At last Dad said, sententiously, "Isn't it true that there are those for whom the climax of their lives was a home run in Little League or something like that ... and that's all they ever reminisce about for the rest of their lives?"

I took the hint. I'd done an incredible thing. I wasn't too sure how I'd brought it off. But it was time to go on now. The train ride was about over and soon we'd be in the real world, terra firma. "Yeah, Dad, I said.

He said, *"La commedia è finita."*

I said, "You so remind me of a fucking wop."

I slipped out before he could embrace me. The smell of death still clung to him a little. Perhaps it would never go away. I ran to the corridor, to the window, to watch the fields unreel.

— *Arlington, Virginia, 1982*

DARKER ANGELS

This, the last story in this little collection, is also the most recent, having only been written a few months ago, in April 1991. (This book therefore spans twelve years of my life ... a complete Asian astrological cycle.) Ed Kramer, editor of a formidable anthology of fantastic stories concerning the Civil War, challenged me to a write a "southern" story. Since Thailand lies well south of the Mason-Dixon line, I decided to try to oblige him.

To my surprise, I found myself returning, for the fourth time in my career, to the theme of this collection. This time I felt a compulsion to write about the terrible, unfeeling things fathers and sons can do to each other, and about the need for forgiveness and atonement. It is the things done to us in childhood that we suffer from the most, though few of us will have undergone the kind of torment the young protagonist of Darker Angels *has seen. But unless we are ready to forgive these wrongs — minor and major — we will always remain prisoners of our childhood.*

This is the first time this story appears in print.

E má shìkà l'aiyé nitori à ní òrun,
a ba dè bodè e o ròjo.

Do not be cruel in this world; for in the
hereafter we go to heaven
    And if we reach the entrance to that place we
will have to argue our case.

— Yoruba sacred song

DARKER ANGELS

One day there'll be historians who can name all the battles and number the dead. They'll study the tactics of the generals and they'll see it all clear as crystal, like they was watching with the eyes of the angels.

But it warn't like that for me. I can't for the life of me put a name to one blame battle we fought. I had no time to number the dead nor could I see them clearly through the haze of red that swam before my eyes. And when the gore-drenched mist settled into dew, when the dead became visible in their stinking, wormy multitudes, I still could not tell one from another; it was a very sea of torsos, heads, and twisted limbs; the dead was wrapped around one another so close and intimate they was like lovers; didn't matter no more iffen they was ours or theirs.

I do not recollect what made me stay behind. Could be it was losing my last shinplaster on the cockroach races. Could have been the coffee which warn't real coffee at all but parched acorns roasted with bacon fat and ground up with a touch of chicory. Could be it was that my shoes was so wore out from marching that every step I took was like walking acrosst a field of brimstone.

More likely it was just because I was a running away kind of a boy. Running was in my blood. My pa and me, we done our share of running, and I reckon that even after I done run away from *him* and gone to war, the running fever was still inside of me and couldn't be let go.

And then, after I lagged behind, I knowed that if I went back they'd shoot me dead, and if they shot me why then I'd go straight on to the everlasting fire, because we was fighting to protect the laws of God. I just warn't ready for hell yet, not after a mere fourteen years on this mortal earth.

That's why I was tarrying amongst the dead, and that's how I come to meet that old darkie that used to work down at the Anderson place.

The sun was about setting and the place was right rank, because the carrion had had the whole day to bloat up and rot and to call out for the birds and the worms and the flies. But it felt good to walk on dead people because they was softer on my wounded feet. The bodies stretched acrosst a shallow creek and all the way up to the edge of a wood. I didn't know where I was nor where I was going. There warn't much light remaining and I wanted to get somewhere, anywhere, before nightfall. It was getting cold. I took a jacket off of one dead man and a pair of new boots from another but I couldn't get the boots on past them open sores.

You might think it a sin to steal from the dead, but the dead don't have no use for gold and silver. There was scant daylight left for me to rifle through their pockets looking for coins. Warn't much in the way of money on that battlefield. It's usually only us poor folks which gets killed in battle.

It was slippery work wading through the corpses, keeping an eye for something shiny amongst the ripped-up torsos and the sightless heads and the coiling guts. I was near choking to death from the reek of it, and the coat I stole warn't much proof against the cold. I was hungry and I had no notion of where to find provender. And the mist was coming back, and I thought to myself, I'll just take myself a few more coppers and then I'll cross over into the wood and build me a shelter and mayhap a fire. Won't nobody see me, thin as a sapling, quiet as a shadow.

So I started to wade over the creek, which warn't no trouble because there was plenty of bodies to use as stepping stones. I was half way acrosst when I spotted the old nigger under a cottonwood tree, in a circle which was clear of carrion. He had a little fire going and something a-roasting over it. I could hear the crackling above the buzz of the flies and I could smell the cooking fat somewhere behind the stench of putrefying men.

I moved nearer to where he sat. I was blame near fainting by then and ready to kill a body for my supper. He was squatting with his arms around his knees and he was a-rocking back and forth and I thought I could hear him crooning some song to himself, like a lullaby, in a language more kin to French than nigger talk. Odd thing was, I had heard the song before. Mayhap my momma done sung it to me onc't, for she was born out Louisiana way. The more I listened the less I was fixing to kill the old man.

He was old all right. As I crept closer I seen he warn't no threat to me. I still couldn't see his face, because he was turned away from me and looking straight into the setting sun. But I could see he was withered and white-haired and black as the coming night, and seemed like he couldn't even hear me approaching, for he never pricked up his ears though I stood nary a yard or two behind his back, in the shadow of the cottonwood.

That was when he said to me, never looking back, "Why, *bonjour*, Marse Jimmy Lee; I never did think I'd look upon you face again."

And then he turned, and I knew him by the black patch over his right eye.

Lord, it was strange to see him there, in the middle of the valley of the dead. It had been ten years since my pa and me gone up to the Anderson place. Warn't never any call to go back, since it burned to the ground a week after, and old man Anderson died, and his slaves was all sold.

"How did you know it was me?" I asked him. "I was but four years old last time you laid eyes on me."

"Your daddy still a itinerant preacher, Marse Jimmy Lee?" he says.

"I reckon," said I, for I warn't about ready to tell him the truth yet. "I ain't with my pa no more."

"You was always a running away sort of a boy," he said, and offered me a piece of what he was roasting.

"What is it?"

"I don't reckon I ought to tell you."

"I've had possum before. I've had field rat. I'm no stranger to strange flesh." I took a bite of the meat and it was right tasty. But I hadn't had solid food for two days and soon I was a-heaving all over the nearest corpse.

He went back to his crooning song, and I remembered then that I had heard it last from his own lips, that day pa shot momma in the back because she wanted to go with the Choctaw farmer. I can't say I blamed her because leastways the man was a landowner and had four slaves besides. Pa let her pack her bags and walk halfway acrosst the bridge afore he blew her to kingdom come. Then he took my hand and set me up on his horse and took me to the Anderson place, and went I started to squall he slapped me in the face until it were purple and black, saying, between his blows, "She don't deserve your tears. She is a woman taken in adultery; such a woman should be stoned to death, according to the scriptures; a bullet were too good for her. I have exercised my rights according to the law, and iffen I hear one more sob out of you I shall take a hickory to you, for he who spareth the rod loveth not his child." And he drained a flask of bug juice and burped, I did not hear the name of Mary Cox from his lips again for ten long years.

Pa was not a ordained minister but plantation folks reckoned him book-learned enough to preach to their darkies, which is what he done every Sunday, a different estate each week, then luncheon with the master and mistress of the house or sometimes, if they was particular about eating with white trash, then in the kitchen amongst the house niggers. The niggers called him the Reverend Cox, but to the white folks he was just Cox, or Bug-juice Cox, or Blame-Fuckster Cox, or wretched, pitiable Cox, so low that his wife done left him for a Injun.

At the Anderson place he preached in a barn, and he took for his subject adultery; and as there was no one to notice, I stole away to a field and sat me down in a thicket of sugar cane and hollered and carried on like the end of the world was nigh, and me just four years old.

Then it was that I heard the selfsame song I was hearing now, and I looked up and saw this ancient nigger with a patch over one eye, and he says to me, "Oh, honey, it be a terrible thing to be without a mother." I remember the smell of him, a pungent smell like fresh crushed herbs. "I still remembers the day my *mamman* was took from me. Oh, do not grieve alone, white child."

"How'd you come to lose that eye?"

"It the price of knowledge, honey," he said softly.

Choking back my sobs, a mite embarrassed because someone had seen me in my loneliness, I said to him, "You shouldn't be here. You should be in that barn listening to my father's preaching, lessen you want to get yourself a whupping."

He smiled sadly and said, "They done given up on whupping old Joseph."

I said, "Is your momma dead too, Joseph?"

"Yes. She be dead, oh, nigh on sixty year now. She died in the revolution."

"Oh, come," I said, "even I know that the revolution was almost a hundred years ago, and I know you ain't that old, because a white man's time is threescore years and ten, and a nigger's time is shorter still." Now I wasn't comprehending anything I was saying; this was all things I heard my pa say, over and over again, in his sermons.

"Oh," said old Joseph, "I ain't talking about the white man's revolution, but the colored folks' revolt which happened on a island name of Haiti. The French, they tortured my *mamman*, but she wouldn't betray her friends, so they killed her and sold me to a slaver, and the ship set sail one day before independence; so sixty years after my kinfolk was set free, I's still in bondage in a foreign country."

I knew that niggers was always full of stories about magic and distant countries, and they couldn't always see truth from fantasy; my daddy told me that truth is a hard, solid thing to us white folks, as easy to grasp as a stone or a horseshoe, but to them it was slippery, it was like a phantom. That was why I

didn't take exception to the old man's lies. I just sat
there quietly, listening to the music of his voice, and
it soothed me and seemed like it helped to salve the
pain I was feeling, for pretty soon when I thought of
momma lying on the bridge choking on her own
blood I felt I could remember the things I loved
about her too, like the way she called my name, the
way her nipples tasted on my lips, for she had lost
my newborn sister and she was bursting with milk
and she would sometimes let me suckle, for all that I
was four years old.

And then I was crying again but this time they
was healing tears.

Then old Joseph, he said, "You listen to me, Marse
Jimmy Lee. I ain't always gone be with you when
you needs to open up your heart." Now this
surprised me because I didn't recollect telling him
none of what was going through my mind. "I's gone
give you a gift," he said, and he pulls out a bottle
from his sleeve, a vial, only a inch high, and in that
bottle was a doll that was woven out of cornstalks. It
were cunningly wrought, for the head of the doll
was bigger than the neck of the bottle, and it must
have taken somebody many hours to make, and
somebody with keen eyesight at that. "Now this be
a problem doll. It can listen to you when no man
will listen. It a powerful magic from the island
where I was born."

He held it out to me and it made me smile, for I
had oftentimes been told that darkies are simple
people and believe in all kinds of magic. I clutched it

in my hands but mayhap he saw the disbelief in my face, for he said to me with the utmost gravity, "Do not mock this magic, white child. Among the colored people which still fears the old gods, they calls me a *houngan,* a man of power."

"The old gods?" I said.

"Shangó," he said, and he done a curious sort of a genuflecting hop when he said the name, "Obatala; Ogun; Babalu Ayé...."

The names churned round and round in my head as I stared into his good eye. I don't recollect what followed next or how my pa found me. But everything else I remembered just as though the ten years that followed, the years of wandering, pa's worsening cruelty and drunkenness, hadn't never even happened.

It was as though I had circled back to that same place and time. Only instead of the burning sunlight of that summer's day there was the gathering cold and the night. Instead of the tall cane sticky with syrup, we was keeping company with the slain. And I warn't a child no more, although I warn't a man yet, neither.

"The *poupée* I give you," old Joseph said as I sat myself down beside him, "does you still got it?"

"My pa found it the next day. He said he didn't want no hoodoo devil dolls in his house. He done smashed it and throwed it in the fire, and then he done wore me out with his hickory."

"And you a soldier now."

"I run away."

"Lordy, honey, you a sight to see. Old Joseph don't got no more dolls for you now. Old Joseph got no time for he be making dolls. There be a monstrous magic abroad now in this universe. This magic it the onliest reason old Joseph still living in this world. Old Joseph hears the magic summoning him. Old Joseph he stay behind to hear what the magic it have to tell him."

Like a fool, I thought him simple when I heard him speak of magic. It made me smile. It was the first time I had smiled in many months. I smiled to keep from crying, for weeping ill becomes a man of fourteen years who has carried his rifle into battle to defend his country.

"You poor lost child," said Joseph, "you should be a-waking up mornings to the song of the larks, not the whistle of miniés nor the thunder of cannon. You at the end of the road now, ain't nowhere left for you to go; that's why us has been called here to this valley of the shadow of death. It was written from the moment we met, Marse Jimmy Lee. Ten years I wandered alone in the wilderness. Now the darker angels has sent you to me."

"I don't know what you mean."

"Be not afraid," he said, "for I bring you glad tidings of great joy." I marveled that he knew the words of the evangelist, for this was the man who would not go hear my father's preaching.

He nibbled at the charred meat. For a moment I entertained the suspicion that it were human flesh. But it smelled good. I ate my fill and drank from the bloody stream and fell asleep beside the fire to the lilt of the old man's lullaby.

***

I had not told old Joseph all the truth. It warn't only the need to run that forced me from my father's house. Pa was a hard man and a drinking man and a man which had visions, and in those visions he saw other worlds. He was unmerciful to me, and oftentimes he would set to whipping the demons out of me, but everything he did to me was in keeping with holy scripture, which tells a father that love ain't always a sweet thing, but can also come with bitterness and blows.

I had visions too, but they warn't heavenly the way his was. I would not wear my shoes. I played with the nigger children of the town, shaming him. I ran wild and I never went to no school. But I could read some, for that my pa set me to studying the scriptures whenever he could tie be down.

This is how I come to join the regiment:

We was living in a shack in back of the Jackson place, right next to the nigger burial plot. Young Master Jackson had all his darkies assembled in the graveyard to hear a special sermon from my pa, because the rumors of the 'mancipation proclamation was rife amongst the slaves. There was maybe thirty or forty of them, and a scattering of pickaninnies underfoot, sitting on the grass, leaning against the wooden markers.

I was sitting in the shack, minding a kettle of stew. Through the open window I could hear my pa preaching. "Now don't you darkies pay this emancipation proclamation no mind," came his voice, ringing and resonant. "It is an evil trickery. There are trying to fool you innocent souls into running away and joining up with those butchers who come down to rape and pillage our land, and they hold out freedom as a reward for treachery. But the true reward is death, for if a nigger is captured in the uniform of a Yankee it has been decreed by our government that he shall be shot without trial. No, this is no road to freedom! There is only one way there for those born into bondage, and that is through the blood of our savior Jesus Christ, and your freedom is not for this world, but for the next, for is it not written, 'In my father's house there are many mansions?' There is a mansion for you, and you, and you, and you, iffen you will obey your master in this life and accept the yoke of lowliness and the lash of repentance; for is it not written, 'By his stripes we are healed' and 'Blessed are the meek'? It's not for the colored people, freedom in this world. But the wicked, compassionless Yankees would prey on your simplicity. They would let you mistake the kingdom of heaven for a rebellious kingdom on earth. 'To everything there is a season.' Yes, there will be mansions for you all. Mansions with white stone columns and porticoes sheltered from the sun. The place of healing is beyond the valley of the shadow of death...."

My pa could talk mighty proper when he had a
mind to, and he had a chapter and verse for
everything. I didn't pay no heed to his words,
though, because there is different chapters and
verses for niggers, and when they are quoted for
white folks they do not always mean the same thing.
No, I was busy stirring the stew and hiding the
whisky, for pa had always had a powerful thirst after
he was done preaching, and with the quenching of
thirst came violence.

After the preaching the darkies all starts singing
with a passion. They done sung *All God's Chillun Got
Wings* and *Swing Low, Sweet Chariot*. Pa didn't stay
for the singing but come into the shack calling for his
food. It warn't ready so he throwed a few pots and
pans around, with me scurrying out of the way to
avoid being knocked about, and then he finally
found where I had hidden the bottle and he
lumbered into the inner room to drink.

Presently the stew bubbled up and I ladled out
some in a tin cup and took it to the room. This was
the room me and him slept in, on a straw pallet on
the floor, a bare room with nothing but a chest of
drawers, a chair with one leg missing, and a hunting
rifle. He kept his hickories there too, for to chastise
me with.

I should have knocked, because pa warn't
expecting me.

He was sitting in the chair with this britches about
his ankles. He didn't see me. He was holding in one
hand a locket which had a picture of momma. In the

other hand he was holding his bony cocker, and he was strenuously indulging in the vice of Onan.

I was right horrified when I saw this. I was full of shame to see my father unclothed, for was that not the shame of the sons of Noah? And I was angered, because in my mind's eye I seen my momma go down on that bridge, fold up and topple over, something I hadn't thought on for nigh on ten year. I stood there blushing scarlet and full of fury and grieving for my dead mother, and then I heard him a-murmuring, "Oh, sweet Jehovah, Oh, sweet Lord, I see you, I see the company of the heavenly host, I see you, my sweet Mary, standing on a cloud with your arms stretched out to me, naked as Eve in the Garden of Eden. Oh, oh, oh, I'm a-looking on the face of the Almighty and a–listening to the song of the angels."

Something broke inside me all at once when I heard him talk that way about momma. Warn't it enough that she was dead, withouten him blasphemously lusting after her departed soul? I dropped the tin of stew and he saw me and I could see the rage burning in his eyes, and I tried to force myself to obey the fifth commandment, but words just came pouring out of me. "Shame on you, pa, pounding your cocker for a woman you done gunned down in cold blood. Don't you think I don't remember the way you kilt her, shot her in the back whilst she were crossing that bridge, and the Choctaw watching on t'other side in his top hat and morning dress, with his four slaves behind him, waiting to take her home."

My pa was silent for a few moments, and the room was filled with the caterwauling of the niggers from the graveyard. We stood there staring each other down. Then he grabbed me by the scruff of the neck and dragged me over to the chair, lurching and stumbling because he hadn't even bothered to pull his britches back up, and I could smell the liquor on him; and he murmured, "You are right; I have sinned; I have sinned; but it is for the son to take on the sins of the world; the paschal lamb; you, Jimmy Lee; oh, God, but you do resemble her; you do remind me of her; oh, it is a heavy burden for you, my son, to take on the sins of the world, but I know that you do it for love," and suchlike, and he reached for the hickory and stripped the shirt off of my back and began to lay to with a will, all the while crying out, "Oh, Mary, oh, my Mary, I am so sorry that you left me ... oh, my son, you shall bear thirty-nine stripes on your back in memory of our savior ... oh, you shall redeem me ..." and the hickory sang and I cried out, not so much from the pain, for that my back was become like leather from long abuse, and warn't much feeling left in it ... I gritted my teeth and try to bear it like I borne it so many times before, but this time it was not to be borne, and when the thirty-ninth stripe was inflicted I tore myself loose from the chair and I screamed, "You ain't hurting me no more, because I ain't no paschal lamb and your sins is *your* sins, not mine," and I pushed him aside with all my strength.

"God, God," he says in a whisper, "I see God." And he rolls his eyes heavenward, excepting that heaven were a leaky roof made from a few planks left over from the slaves' quarters.

Then I took the rifle from the wall and pounded him in the head with the stock, three, four, five, six times until he done slumped onto the straw.

Oh, I was raging and afeared, and I run away right then and there, without even making sure iffen he was kilt or not. I run right through them darkies, who was a-singing and a-carrying on to wake the very dead; they did not see a scrawny boy, small for his age, slip through them and out toward the woods.

I run and run with three dimes in my pocket and a sheaf of shinplasters that I stole from the chest of drawers, I run and I don't even recollect iffen I put out the fire on the stove.

And that was how I come to be with the regiment, tramping through blood and mud and shitting my bowels away with the flux each day; and that was how I come to be sleeping next to old Joseph, the hoodoo doctor, who become another father to me.
     ***

I did not confess to old Joseph or even to myself that I had done my father in. Mayhap he was still alive. I tried not to think on him. My old life was dead. Surely I could not go back to the Jackson place, nor the army, nor any other place from which I run. There was just me and the old nigger now, scavengers, carrion birds, eaters of the dead.

Yes, and sure it was human flesh old Joseph fed me that night, and again that morning. He showed me the manner of taking it, for there was certain corpses that cried out to be let be, whilst others craved to be consumed. We followed the army a a safe distance, and when they moved on we took possession of the slain. He could always sniff out where a battle was going to be. He never carried nothing with him excepting a human skull, painted black, that was full of herbs, the same herbs that he always smelled of.

Oh, it was God's country we done passed through, hills, forests, meadows, creeks, and all this beauty marred by the handiwork of men. Old Joseph showed me not to drink from the bloodied streams but to lick the dew from flower petals and cupped leaves of a morning. As his trust of me grew, he became more bold. We went into encampments and sat amongst the soldiers, and they never seen us, not once.

"We is invisible," old Joseph told me.

And then it struck me, for we stood in broad daylight beside a willow tree, and on the other side of the brook was mayhap fifty tents and behind them a dense wood. The air was moist and thick. I could see members of my old company, with their skull faces too small for their gray coats, barely able to lift their bayonets off the ground, and they was sitting

there huddled together waiting for gruel, but there I
was, nourished by the dead, my flesh starting to fill
out and the redness back in my cheeks; it struck me
that they couldn't see me even though I was a-
jumping up and down on the other side of the
stream; and I said to old Joseph, "I don't think we
are invisible. I think ... oh, old Joseph, I think we
have been dead ever since the day we met."

Old Joseph laughed; it were a dry laugh, like the
wind stirring the leaves in autumn; and he said,
"You ain't dead yet, honey; feel the flesh on them
bones; no, your *beau-père* he nurturing you back to
life."

"Then why don't they see us? Even when we
walk amongst them?"

"Because I has cast a cloak of darkness about us.
We be wearing the face of a dark god over our own."

"I don't trust God. Whenever my pa seen God, he
hurt me."

Smiling, he said, "You daddy warn't a true
preacher, honey; he just a *houngan macoute*, a man
which *use* the name of God to adorn hisself."

And taking my hand he led me acrosst that
branch and we was right amongst the soldiers, and
still they did not see me. We helped ourselves to
hardtack and coffee right out of the kettle. In the
distance I heard the screams of a man whose leg they
was fixing to hack off. Around us men lay moaning.
There is a sick-sweet body smell that starving men
give off when they are burning up their last shreds of
flesh to fuel their final days. That's how I knew they

was near death. They was shivering with cold, even though it were broad daylight. Lord, many of them was just children, and some still younger than myself. I knew that the war was lost, or soon would be. I had no country, and no father save for a darkie witch doctor from Haiti.

There come a bugle call and a few men looked up, though most of them just goes on laying in their misery. Old Joseph and I saw soldiers come into the camp. They had a passel of niggers with them, niggers in blue uniforms, all chained up in a long row behind a wagon that was piled high with confiscated arms. They was as starved and miserable as our own men. They stared ahead as they trudged out of the wood and into the clearing. There was one or two white men with them two, officers I reckoned.

A pause, and the bugle sounded again. Then a captain come out of a tent and addressed the captives. He said, in a lugubrious voice, as though he were weary of making this announcement: "According to the orders given me by the congress of the Confederate States of America, all Negroes apprehended while in the uniform of the North are not to be considered prisoners of war, but shall be returned instantly to a condition of slavery or shot. Any white officer arrested while in command of such Negroes shall be considered to be inciting rebellion and also shot." He turned and went back into his tent, and the convoy moved onward, past the camp, upstream, toward another part of the woods.

"*Oba kosó!*" the old man whispered. "They gone kill them."

"Let's go away," I said.

"No," said old Joseph, "I feels the wind of the gods blowing down upon me. I feels the breath of the loa. I is standing on the coils of Koulèv, the earth-serpent. Oh, no, Marse Jimmy Lee, I don't be going nowhere, but you free to come and go as you pleases of course, being white."

"You know that ain't so," I said. "I'm less free than you. And I know if I leave you I will leave the shelter of your invisibility spell." For that I gazed right into the eyes of the prisoners, and tasted their rancid breath, and smelled the pus of their wounds, and seen no sign of recognition. There was something to his magic, though that I was sure it come of the dark places, and not of God.

So I followed him alongside the creek as the captives were led into the wood, followed them uphill a ways until we reached the edge of a shallow gully, and there was already niggers there, digging to make it deeper, and I seen what was going to happen and I didn't want to look, because this warn't a battle, this were butchery pure and simple.

Our soldiers didn't mock the prisoners and didn't call them no names. They were too tired and too hungry. The blacks and the whites, they didn't show no passion in their faces. They just wanted it to end. Our men done lined the niggers and their officers up all along the edge of the ditch, and searched through their pockets for any coins or crumbs, and they turned them so they faced the gully and they done shot them in the back, one by one, until the pit was filled; then the Southerners turned and filed back to the camp. Oh, God! As the first shots rung out it put me in mind of my mother Mary, halfway across the bridge, with her old life behind her and her new life ahead of her, dead on her face, and the bloodstain spreading from her back on to the lace and calico.

And old Joseph said, "Honey, I seen what I must do. And it a dark journey that I must take, and maybe you don't be strong enough to come with me. But I hates to journey alone. Old Joseph afraid too, betimes, spite of his 'leventy-leven years upon this earth. I calls the powers to witness, *ni ayé àti ni òrun.*"

"What does that mean, old Joseph?"

"In heaven as it is in earth."

I saw the way his eye glowed and I was powerful afraid. He had become more than a shrunken old man. Seemed like he drew the sun's light into his face and shone brighter than the summer sky. He set his cauldron-skull down on the ground and said, again and again, *"Koulèv, Koulèv-O! Damballah Wedo, Papa! Koulèv, Koulèv-O! Damballah Wedo, Papa!"*

And then he says, in a raspy voice, "Watch out, Marse Jimmy Lee, the god gone come down and mount my body now … stand clear less you wants to swept away by the breath of the serpent!" And he mutters to hisself, "Oh, *dieux puissants,* why you axing me to make biggest magic, me a old magician without no *poudre* and no herbs? Oh, take this cup from me, take, take this bitter poison from he lips, for old Joseph he don't study life and death no more."

And his old body started to shake, and he ripped off his patch and threw it onto the mud, and I looked into the empty eye-socket and saw an inner eye, blood-red and shiny as a ruby. And he sank down on his knees in front of the pit of dead men and he went on a-mumbling and a-rocking, back and forth, back and forth, and seemed like he was a-speaking in tongues. And his good eye rolled right up into its socket.

"Why, old Joseph," I says to him, "what are you fixing to do?"

But he paid me no mind. He just went on a-shimmying and a-shaking, and presently he rose up from where he was and started to dance a curious hopping sort of dance, and with every hop he cried, *"Shangó! Shangó!"* in a voice that was steadily losing its human qualities. And soon his voice was rolling like thunder, and presently it *was* the thunder, for the sky was lowering and lightning was lancing the cloud-peaks.

Oh, the sky became dark. The cauldron seethed and glowed, though he hadn't even touched it. I knew he were sure possessed. The dark angels he done told me of, they was speaking to him out of the mouth of hell.

I reckoned I was not long for this world, for the old man was a-hollering at the top of his lungs and we warn't far from the encampment; but no one came looking for us. Mayhap they was huddled in their tents hiding from the thunder. Presently it began to rain, it pelted us and soaked us, that rain; it were a hot rain, scalding to my skin. And when the lightning flashed I looked into the pit and I thought I saw something moving. Mayhap it were just the rushing waters, throwing the corpses one against t'other. I crept closer to the edge of the gully. I didn't heed old Joseph's warning. I peered over the edge and in the next flash of lightning I saw them a-writhing and a-shaking their arms and legs, and their necks a-craning this way and that, and I thought to myself, old Joseph he is raising the dead.

Old Joseph just went on screaming out those African words and leaping up and waving his arms. The rain battered my body and I was near fainting from it, for the water flooded my nostrils and drenched my lungs and when I gasped for air I swallowed more and more water; I don't know how the old man kept on dancing; in the lightning flashes I saw him, dark and lithe, and the sluicing rain made him glisten and made his chest and arms to look like the scales of a great black serpent; I looked on him and breathed in the burning water, and the pit of dead niggers quook as iffen the very earth were opening up, and there come a blue light from the mass grave, so blinding that I could see no more; and so, at last, I passed out from the terror of it.

***

When I done opened my eyes the rain was just a memory; the sun was rising; the forest was silent and shrouded in mist. And I thought to myself, I have been dreaming, and I am still beside the creek where the dead bodies lay, and I never did see no old Joseph out of my past; but then I saw him frying up a bit of salt pork he done salvaged from the camp. Warn't no morning bugle calls, and I reckon the company done up and gone in the middle of the night, soon as the storm subsided.

Old Joseph, the patch was over his eye again, and he was singing to hisself, that song I heard as a child. And when he saw me stir, he said, "Marse Jimmy Lee, you awake now."

"What is that song?" I asked him.

"It called *Au Claire de la Lune,* honey; 'by the light of the moon.'"

I sat up. "Joseph?"

"What, Marse Jimmy Lee?"

"Last night I had the strangest dream ... more like a vision. I dreamed you were possessed, and you pranced about and waved your arms and sang songs in a African language, and you raised up nigger soldiers from the grave."

"Life is a dream, honey," he says, "we calls them *les zombis.* It from a Kikongo word nzambi that mean a dead man that walk the earth."

The fog began to clear a little and I saw their feet. Black feet, still shackled, still covered with chafing sores. We was surrounded by them. And as the sunlight began to dissipate the mist, I could see their faces; it was them which had been kilt and buried in the pit; I knew some of their faces. For though they stirred, they moved, they looked about them, there were no fire in their eyes, and didn't have no breath in their nostrils. Mayhap they wasn't dead, but they wasn't alive, neither.

The stood there, looming over us. Each one with a wound clean through him. Each one smelling of old Joseph's herbs.

"The magic still in me," old Joseph said, "even without the *coup poudre*."

I reckon I have never been more scared than I was then. My skin was crawling and my blood was racing.

"I never thought that old magic still in me," said Joseph again. There was wonderment in his voice. No fear. The dead men surrounded us, waiting; seemed like they had no mind of their own.

"Oh, Joseph, what are we going to do?"

"Don't know, white child. I's still in the dark. The vision don't come as clear to me no more; old Joseph he old, he old."

He fed me and gave me genuine coffee to drink, for the slain Yankees had carried some with them. I rose and went over to the pit, and it were sure enough empty save for the two white officers. "Why didn't you raise them too?" I said.

"Warn't no sense in it, Marse Jimmy Lee; for white folks there is a heaven and a hell; there ain't no middle ground; best to forget them."

So we threw dirt over them and we marched on, and the column of undead darkies followed us. I could not name the places that we passed, but old Joseph knew where he was going. It was toward the rising sun so I guessed it was south.

At nightfall we rested. We found a farmhouse. There warn't no people and the animals was all took away, but I found a ham a-hanging in the larder, and I feasted. In the night I slept in a real bed. Old Joseph sat out on the porch. The *zombis* did not sleep. The stood in a ring outside the house and the swayed softly to the sound of Joseph's singing; as I looked out of the smashed window I could see them in the moonlight, and there was still no fire in their eyes; and I recollected that they hadn't partaken of no victuals. What was it like to be a *zombi?* Iffen that the eyes are the windows of the soul, then surely there warn't no souls inside those fleshy shells.

We found plenty of gold in the abandoned house, they done hid it in a well, which was surrounded by dead Yankees; I reckon they done poisoned it so that the northerners wouldn't be able to drink their water. But poison means naught to the dead.

And we walked on; and the passel of walking dead became a company, for wherever we went we found niggers that had been kilt, not just the ones in Yankee uniform but sometimes a woman lying dead in a ditch, or a young buck chained to a tree that was just abandoned and let starve to death when his masters fled from the enemy, and one time we found seven high-yaller children dead in a cage, with gunshot wounds to their heads; for they was frenzied times, and men were driven to acts not thought upon in times of peace. It was amongst the dead children that I found another cornstalk *poupée* like the one old Joseph gave me ten years before, a-sitting in a vial in the clenched fist of a dead little girl; after we done wakened them, she held it out to me, and I thought there were a glimmer in her eye, but mayhap it were only my imagination.

"Get up and walk," old Joseph said. And they walked.

And I said over and over to him, "Old Joseph, where are we going?"

And he said, "Towards freedom."

"But freedom is in the north, ain't it?"

"Freedom in the heart, honey."

We marched. For many days we didn't see no white folks at all. We saw burned hulks of farms, and stray dogs hunting in packs. We passed other great battlefields, and them that was worth reviving, that still had enough flesh on them to be able to march, old Joseph raised up. He was growing in power. It got so he would just wave his hands, and say one or two words, and the dead man would climb right out of the ground. And I took to repeating the words to myself, soundlessly at first, just moving my lips; then softly, then — for when he were a-concentrating on his magic, he couldn't see nothing of the world — I would shout out those words along with him, I would wrap my tongue around them twisted and barbarian sounds, and I would tell myself, 'twas I which raised them, I which reached into the abyss and drawed them out.

Still we encountered no sign of human life. The summer sun streamed down on us by day and seemed like I sweat blood. It warn't at all certain to me that we was still alive and on this earth, for the land was a waste land, spite of the verdant meadows and the mountains blanketed with purple flowers, spite of the rich-smelling earth and the warm rain. Sometimes I think that the country we was wandering in was an illusion, a false Eden. Or that we was somehow half in, half out of the world.

Though I didn't know where the road was leading, yet I was happy. I trusted old Joseph, and I didn't have no one else left in the world. The only times I become sad was thinking on my pa and momma's death, and wondering iffen my pa was with God now, for he said he done seen the face of God before I smashed his head. Sometimes I dreamed about coming home to see him well again. But they was only dreams. I knew that I had kilt him.

On the seventh day we come onc't more into the sight of men.

***

The road become wider and we was coming into the vicinity of a town. I knew this was a port, maybe Charleston. There warn't no signs to tell us, but pa and I had been booted out of Charleston once, I remembered the way the wind smelt, wet and tangy.

A few miles outside town our road joined up with a wider road that come in a straight line from due north. On the other road, straggling down to meet us, we saw a company of graycoats.

Not many of them, maybe three dozen. They warn't exactly marching. Some was leaning on each other, some hobbling, and one, a slip of a boy, tapped on the side of a skinless drum. Their clothes was in tatters and most of them didn't have no rifles. They was just old men and boys, for the able-bodied had long since fallen.

They seen us and one of them cried out, "Nigger soldiers!" They fell into a pathetic semblance of a formation, and them which had rifles aimed them and them which had crutches brandished them at us.

I shouted out, "Let us pass ... we don't have no quarrel with you." For they were wretched creatures, these remnants of the Southern army, and I was sure that the war was already lost, and they was coming back to what was left of their homes.

But one boy, mayhap their leader, screamed at me, "Nigger lover! Traitor!" I looked in his eyes and saw we were just alike, poor trash fighting a rich man's war, him and me; and I pitied the deluded soul. Because I knew now that there warn't no justice in this war, and that neither side had foughten for God, but only for hisself.

"It's no use!" I shouted at the boy who was so like myself. "These darkies ain't even alive; they're shadows marching to the sea; they ain't got souls to kill."

And old Joseph said, "March on, my children."

They commenced to fire on us.

This was the terriblest thing which I did witness on that journey. For the nigger soldiers marched and marched, and not a bullet could stop them. The miniés flew and the white boys shrieked out a ghostly echo of a rebel yell, and *les zombis* kept right on coming and coming, and me and old Joseph with them, untouched by the bullets, for his magic still shielded our mortal flesh. The niggers marched. Their faces was ripped asunder and still they marched. Their brains came oozing from their skulls, their guts came writhing from their bellies, and still they marched. They marched until they were too close for bullets. Then the white boys flung themselves at us, and they was ripped to pieces. They was tore limb from limb by dead men which stared with glazed and vacant eyes. It took but a few minutes, this final skirmish of the war. Their yells died in their throats. The *zombis* broke their necks and flung them to the ground. Their strength warn't a human kind of strength. They'd shove their hands into an old man's belly and snap his spine and pull out the intestines like a coil of rope. They'd take a rifle and break the barrel in two.

There was no anger in what the *zombis* done. And they didn't make no noise whilst they was killing. They done it the way you might darn a sock or feed the chickens; it were just something which had to be done.

And we marched onward, leaving the bodies to rot; it was getting on toward sunset now.

Oh, I was angry. The boys we kilt warn't no strangers from the north; they could have been my brothers. Oh, I screamed in rage at old Joseph; I didn't trust him no more; the happiness had left me.

"Did you hear what he called me?" I shouted. "A traitor to my people. A nigger lover. And it's God's plain truth. If you wanted freedom why didn't you go north into the arms of the Yankees? You spoke to me of a big magic, and of the coils of the serpent Koulèv, and the wind of the gods, and the voices of darker angels ... to what end? It were Satan's magic, magic to give the dead an illusion of life, so you could kill more of my people!"

"Be still," he said to me, as the church spires of the port town rose up in the distance. "Your war don't be my war. You think the Yankees got theyselfs kilt to set old Joseph free? You think the 'mancipation proclamation was wrote to give the nigger back he soul? I say to you, white child, that a piece of paper don't make men free. The black man in this land he ain't gone be free tomorrow nor in a hundred years nor in a thousand. I didn't bring men back from the outer darkness so they could shine you shoes and wipe you butts. The army I lead, he kingdom don't be of this earth."

"You are mad, old Joseph," I said, and I wept, for he was no longer a father to me.

***

We marched into the town. Children peered from behind empty beer kegs with solemn eyes. Horses reared up and whinnied. Women stared sullenly at us. The Yankees had already took the town, and half the houses was smoldering, and we didn't see no grown men. The stars and stripes flew over the ruint courthouse. I reckon folks thought we was just another company of the conquering army.

We reached the harbor. There was one or two sailing ships docked there; rickety ships with tattered sails. The army of dead men stood at attention and old Joseph said to me: "Now I understands why you come with me so far. There a higher purpose to everything, *ni ayé àti ni òrun.*"

I didn't want to stay with him any more. When I seen the way *les zombis* plowed down my countrymen, I had been moved to a powerful rage, and the rage would not die away. "What higher purpose?" I said. And the salt wind chafed my lips.

"You think," said old Joseph, "that old Joseph done tricked you, he done magicked you with mirrors and smoke; but I never told you we was fighting on the same side. But we come far together, and I wants you to do me one last favor afore we parts for all eternity."

"And what sort of favor would that be, old sorcerer? I thought you could do anything."

"Anything. But not this thing. You see, old Joseph a nigger. Nigger he can't go into no portside bar to offer gold for to buy him a ship."

"You want a ship now? Where are you fixing to go? Back to Haiti, where the white man rules no more?"

Old Joseph said, "Mayhap it a kind of Haiti where we go." He laughed. "Haiti, yes, Haiti! And I gone see my dear *mamman,* though she be cold in her grave sixty year past. Or mayhap it mother Africa herself we go to. *Oba kosó!"*

And I remembered that he had told me: *My kingdom is not of this earth.* He had used the words of our savior and our Lord. Oh, the ocean wind were warm, and it howled, and the torn sails clattered against the masts. The air fair dripped with moisture. And the niggers stood like statues, all-unseeing.

"I'll do as you ask," I said, and I took the sack of gold we had gathered from the poisoned well, and I walked along the harbor until I found a bar and ship's captain for hire, which was not hard, for the embargo had starved their business. And presently I come back and told old Joseph everything was ready. And the niggers lined up, ready to embark. Night was falling.

But as they prepared themselves to board that ship, I could hold my tongue no more. "Old Joseph," I said, "your kingdom is founded on a lie. You have waked these bodies from the earth, but where are their souls? You may dream of leading these creatures to a mystic land acrosst the sea, and you may dream of freeing them forever from the bonds of servitude, but how can you free what can't be freed? How can you free a rock, a tree, a piece of earth? Dust they were and dust they ever shall be, world without end."

And the zombi warriors stood, unmoving and unblinking, and not a breath passed their lips, though that the wind was rising and whipping at our faces.

And old Joseph looked at me long and hard, and I knew that I had said the thing that must be said. He whispered, "Out of the mouths of babes and sucklings hast thou ordained strength, O Lord." He fell down on his knees before me and said, "And all this time I thought that *I* the wise one and you the student! Oh, Marse Jimmy Lee, you done spoke right. There be no life in *les zombis* because I daresn't pay the final price. But now I's *gone* make that sacrifice. Onc't I done gave my eye in exchange for knowledge. But there be *two* trees in Eden, Marse Jimmy Lee; there be the tree of knowledge, and there be the tree of life."

So saying he covered his face with his hands. He plunged his thumb into the socket of his good eye and he plucked it out, screaming to almighty God with the pain of it. His agony was real. His shrieking curdled my blood. It brought back my pa's chastisements and my momma's dying and the tramping of my bare feet on sharp stones and the sight of all my comrades, pierced through by bayonets, cloven by cannon, their limbs ripped off, their bellies torn asunder, their lives gushing hot and young and crimson into the stream. Oh, but I craved to carry his pain, but he were the one that were chosen to bear it, and I was the one which brung him to the understanding of it.

And now his eye were in his hand, a round, white, glistening pearl, and he cries out in a thunderous voice, "If thine eye offend thee, pluck it out!" and he takes blind aim and hurls the eye with all his might into the mighty sea.

I clenched the *poupée* in my hand.

Then came lightning, for old Joseph had summoned the power of the serpent Koulèv, whose coils were entwined about the earth. Then did he unleash the rain. Then did he turn to me, with the gore gushing from the yawning socket, and cry to me, a good-for-nothing white trash boy which kilt his own father and stole from the dead, "Thou hast redeemed me."

Then, and only then, did I see the *zombis* smile. Then, as the rain softened, as the sky did glow with a cold blue light that didn't come from no sun nor moon, then did hear the laughter of the dead, and the fire of life begin to flicker in their eyes. But they was already trooping up the gangplank, and presently there was only the old man, purblind now, and like to die I thought.

"Farewell," he says to me.

And I said, "No, old Joseph. You are blind now. You need a boy to hold your hand and guide you, to be your eyes against the wild blue sea."

"Not blind," he said. "I *chooses* not to see. I gone evermore be looking inward, at the glory and the majesty of eternal light."

"But what have I?" Where can I go, excepting that I go with you?"

"Honey, you has lived but fourteen of your threescore and ten. It don't be written that you's to follow a old man acrosst the sea to a land that maybe don't even *be* a land save in that old man's dream. Go now. But first you gone kiss your *beau-père* goodbye, for I loves you."

My tears were brine and his were blood. As I kissed his cheek the salt did run together with the crimson. I saw him no more; I did not see the ship sail from the port; for my eyes was blinded with weeping.

***

So I walked and walked and walked until I come back to the Jackson place. The mansion were a cinder, and even the fields was all burnt up, and the animals was dead. The place was looted good and thorough; warn't one thing of value in the vicinity, not a gold piece nor a silver spoon nor even the rugs that the Jacksons done bought from a French merchant.

I walked up the low knoll to where the nigger graveyard was and where our shack onc't stood. The wooden markers was all charred, and here and there was a shred of homespun clinging to them; and I thought to myself, mayhap the Yankees come down to the Jackson place not an hour after I done run away, whilst the slaves was still a-singing their spirituals. That cloth was surely torn off some of the slave women, for the Yankees loved to have their way with darkies. And I thought, mayhap my pa is still laying inside that shack, in the inner room, beside the locket with mamma's picture, with his hickory in his fist, with his britches down about his ankles.

And so it was I found him.

He warn't rank no more. It had been many months since I run off. Warn't much left of his face that the worms hadn't ate. At his naked loins, the bone poked through the papery hide, and there was a swarm of ants. It was a miracle there was this much left of him, for there was wild dogs roaming the fields.

I set down the *poupée* on the chair and got to wondering what I should do. What I wanted most in life were a new beginning. I spoke to that doll, for I knew that old Joseph's spirit was in it somehow, and I said, "I don't know where you come from, and I don't know where you are. But oh, give me the strength to begin onc't more, oh, carry me back from the land of the dead."

Without thinking I started to murmur the words of power, the African words I done mimicked when I watched him raise the dead. I knelt down beside the corpse of my pa and waited for the breath of serpent. I whispered them words over and over until my mind emptied itself and was filled with the souls of darker angels.

I reckon I knelt all night long, or mayhap many nights. But when I opened my eyes again there was flesh on my father's bones, and he was beginning to rouse himself; and his eyes had the fire of life, for that old Joseph had sacrificed his second eye.

"You sure have growed, son," he says softly. "You ain't a sapling no more; you're a mighty tree."

"Yes, pa," says I.

"Oh, son, you have carried me back from a terrible dream. In that dream I abandoned you, and I practiced all manner of cruelty upon you, and a dark angel came to you and became your new pa; and you followed him to the edge of the river that divides the quick from the dead."

"Yes, pa. But I stopped at the river bank and watched him sail away. And I come back to you."

"Oh, Jimmy Lee, my son, I have seen hell. I have been down into the fire of damnation, and I've felt the loneliness of perdition. And the cruelest torture was being cut off from you, my flesh and blood. Oh, sweet Jesus, Jimmy Lee, it were only that you made me think on her so much, she which I killed, she which I never loved more even as I sent the bullet flying into her back."

And this was strange, for in the old days my pa had only spoke of heaven, and of seeing the face of God, and when he done seen God he would wear me out, calling on His holy name to witness his infamy and my sacrifice. But now he had seen hell and he was full of gentleness.

And then he said to me, "My son, I craves your forgiveness."

"Ain't nothing to forgive."

"Then give me your love," says he, "for you are tall and strong, and I have become old; and it is now for you to be the father, and I the child."

It were time to cross the bridge. It were time to heal the hurting.

"My love you have always had, pa."

So saying, I embraced him; and thus it was our war came to an end.

— Sun Valley, California, 1993

ABOUT THE AUTHOR

Once referred to by the International Herald Tribune as "the most well-known expatriate Thai in the world," Somtow Sucharitkul is no longer an expatriate, since he has returned to Thailand after five decades of wandering the world. He is best known as an award-winning novelist and a composer of operas.

Born in Bangkok, Somtow grew up in Europe and was educated at Eton and Cambridge. His first career was in music and in the 1970s he acquired a reputation as a revolutionary composer, the first to combine Thai and Western instruments in radical new sonorities. Conditions in the arts in the region at the time proved so traumatic for the young composer that he suffered a major burnout, emigrated to the United States, and reinvented himself as a novelist.

His earliest novels were in the science fiction field but he soon began to cross into other genres. In his 1984 novel Vampire Junction, he injected a new literary inventiveness into the horror genre, in the words of Robert Bloch, author of Psycho, "skilfully combining the styles of Stephen King, William Burroughs, and the author of the Revelation to John." Vampire Junction was voted one of the forty all-time greatest horror books by the Horror Writers' Association, joining established classics like Frankenstein and Dracula.

In the 1990s Somtow became increasingly identified as a uniquely Asian writer with novels such as the semi-autobiographical Jasmine Nights. He won the World Fantasy Award, the highest accolade given in the world of fantastic literature, for his novella The Bird Catcher. His fifty-three books have sold about two million copies world-wide. After becoming a Buddhist monk for a period in 2001, Somtow decided to refocus his attention on the country of his birth, founding Bangkok's first international opera company and returning to music, where he again reinvented himself, this time as a neo-Asian neo-Romantic composer. The Norwegian government commissioned his song cycle Songs Before Dawn for the 100th Anniversary of the Nobel Peace Prize, and he composed at the request of the government of Thailand his Requiem: In Memoriam 9/11 which was dedicated to the victims of the 9/11 tragedy.

According to London's Opera magazine, "in just five years, Somtow has made Bangkok into the operatic hub of Southeast Asia." His operas on Thai themes,*Madana, Mae Naak, Ayodhya,* and *The Silent Prince* have been well received by international critics. His most recent operas, the Japanese inspired *Dan no Ura* and the fantasy opera *The Snow Dragon,* have gained him acceptance as "one of the most intriguing of contemporary opera composers" (Auditorium Magazine). He has recently embarked on a ten-opera cycle, *Dasjati — Ten Lives of the Buddha* - which when completed will be the classical music work with the largest time span and scope in history.

He is increasingly in demand as a conductor specializing in opera and in the late-romantic composers like Mahler. His repertoire runs the entire gamut from Monteverdi to Wagner. His work has been especially lauded for its stylistic authenticity and its lyricism. He has received the "Golden W" from the International Wagner Society. The orchestra he founded in Bangkok, the Siam Philharmonic, mounted the first complete Mahler cycle in the region.

Somtow's current project, the Siam Sinfonietta, is a youth orchestra he founded five years ago, using a new educational method he pioneered and which is now among the most acclaimed youth orchestras world-wide, receiving standing ovations in Carnegie Hall, The Konzerthaus in Berlin, Disney Hall, the Musikverein in Vienna, and many other venues around the world.

He is the first recipient of Thailand's "Distinguished Silpathorn" award, given for an artist who has made and continues to make a major impact on the region's culture, from Thailand's Ministry of Culture.

He is the first Asian (and only the second composer after Hans Werner Henze) to receive the Europa Kultur-Forum's European Cultural Achievement Award.

BOOKS BY S.P. SOMTOW

General Fiction
The Shattered Horse
Jasmine Nights
Forgetting Places
The Other City of Angels (Bluebeard's Castle)
The Stone Buddha's Tears

Dark Fantasy
The Timmy Valentine Series:
>   *Vampire Junction*
>   *Valentine*
>   *Vanitas*

Vampire Junction Special Edition
Moon Dance
Darker Angels
The Vampire's Beautiful Daughter

Science Fiction

Starship & Haiku
Mallworld
The Ultimate Mallworld
The Ultimate, Ultimate, Ultimate Mallworld
Chronicles of the High Inquest:
    Light on the Sound
    The Darkling Wind
    The Throne of Madness
    Utopia Hunters
Chroniques de l'Inquisition - Volume 1 (omnibus)
Chroniques de l'Inquisition - Volume 2 (omnibus)
Inquestor Tales One: The Singing Moons

The Aquiliad Series:
    Aquila in the New World
    Aquila and the Iron Horse
    Aquila and the Sphinx

Fantasy
The Riverrun Trilogy:
    Riverrun
    Armorica
    Yestern
The Riverrun Trilogy (omnibus)
The Fallen Country Wizard's Apprentice
The Snow Dragon (omnibus)

Media Tie-in
The Alien Swordmaster
Symphony of Terror
The Crow - Temple of Night
Star Trek: Do Comets Dream?

Chapbooks
Fiddling for Waterbuffaloes
I Wake from a Dream of a Drowned Star City
A Lap Dance with the Lobster Lady
Compassion — Two Perspectives

Libretti
Mae Naak
Ayodhya
Madana
Dan no Ura
Helena Citronova
The Snow Dragon
Dasjati:
    Temiya - The Silent Prince
    Sama - The Faithful Son
    Bhuridat - The Dragon Lord
    Mahosadha - Architect of Dreams
    Nemiraj - Chariot of Heaven

Collections
My Cold Mad Father
Fire from the Wine Dark Sea
Chui Chai (Thai)
Nova (Thai)
The Pavilion of Frozen Women
Dragon's Fin Soup
Tagging the Moon
Face of Death (Thai)
Other Edens
S.P. Somtow's The Great Tales (Thai)
Terror Nova (in press)
Terror Antiqua (in press)

Essays, Poetry and Miscellanies
Opus Fifty
A Certain Slant of "I" (in press)
Sonnets about Serial Killers
Opera East
Victory in Vienna (ed.)
Three Continents (ed.)
Nirvana Express
Caravaggio x 2
The Maestro's Noctuary